The author's othe

- *"The Perfect Steel Trap Harpers Ferry 1859"* 2006 -- Named a finalist in the 2006 Best Book Awards by USA Book News. E-book.

- *"The Virginian Who Might Have Saved Lincoln"* 2007 – Also available as an Audio Book – Named first-runner up in the 2008 National Indie Excellence Awards for "Audio Books – Fiction" and named finalist in the 2008 Best Book Awards by USA Book News for "Audio Fiction – Unabridged". E-book.

- *"Catesby: Eyewitness to the Civil War"* 2008

- *"The U.S. Colored Troops at Andersonville Prison"* 2009 – Non-Fiction

- *"The Centennial History of Ranson, West Virginia 1910-2010"* 2010

- *"The Life of Abraham Lincoln: As President"* by Ward Hill Lamon and written circa 1880, edited by the author and published for the first time – 2010 – Named finalist in the 2011 National Indie Excellence Awards for History. E-book.

A House Divided Against Itself

By Bob O'Connor

INFINITY
PUBLISHING

Cover artwork – *"My Friend, the Enemy"* by Mort Künstler
© 2008 Mort Künstler, Inc. (www.mortkunstler.com)

ISBN 0-7414-6937-5 Paperback
ISBN 0-7414-6938-3 eBook

Printed in the United States of America

This is an historical novel. All the characters are real persons. The story is based on true incidents in the American Civil War.

Published October 2011

INFINITY PUBLISHING
1094 New DeHaven Street, Suite 100
West Conshohocken, PA 19428-2713
Toll-free (877) BUY BOOK
Local Phone (610) 941-9999
Fax (610) 941-9959
Info@buybooksontheweb.com
www.buybooksontheweb.com

Dedication

To my son, Craig, who has always made me proud.

Foreword

When people discuss the American Civil War, it is often said "brother fought against brother". While it is technically correct that brothers fought on opposite sides in the long conflict, it was only in rare instances that the brothers actually fought against each other at the same battle, on the same day.

However, in rare instances, particularly in the Shenandoah Campaign of the Valley, units pushed each other back and forth, up and down the valley, often fighting against each other multiple times.

The story you are about to read is about several instances in which two brothers, one fighting for the North, the other fighting for the South, were at the same battle at the same time.

They both fought for their own cause. One sought to preserve the Union. The other wanted to protect his homeland from invasion.

Each thought his was the right cause. They both believed they would win in the end.

One brother fought in a Pennsylvania unit that included many of his friends and neighbors from Gettysburg. His brother fought in a Virginia unit that included some of the men who worked alongside him in the carriage business in Shepherdstown.

Each thought the war would be short when he enlisted. Each re-enlisted when the war carried on longer than expected.

The war had divided family and friends. The split between the brothers widened as the conflict escalated. By war's end, one doubted if the house divided against itself would ever be brought back together again.

Part I

The Early Days
John Wesley Culp

I am John Wesley Culp, the second son of Esaias and Margaret Ann Culp. My name comes from the famous religious leader John Wesley who founded the Methodist Church. Most folks call me Wesley. I am twenty-one years old. I am also very small – only around five feet tall.

I was born in Petersburg, Pennsylvania, in 1839. I lived most of my younger years in Gettysburg, Pennsylvania.

William Esaias Culp is my brother. He is about 8 years older than me.

I have two sisters, Barbara Anne (I call her Annie) and Julia. Annie is five years older than me – with Julia about four years younger than me. I know I am not allowed to have favorites, but just between you and me, Annie was my favorite sister. She listened and supported me, even when I was in trouble. And that seemed to be often.

When everyone else was yellin at me, if I looked up, Annie would be winkin and noddin, lettin me know that she was still on my side.

As far back as I can remember, my brother didn't like me much. He picked on me, teased me and called me names. He never quit. Even when mother stepped in and kept him from me, he only stopped long enough to catch his breath.

My best friend in Gettysburg was Johnston Hastings Skelly, Jr. To me he was just plain old Jack Skelly. He and I were wanderers and explorers. We hiked around every inch of Gettysburg and the surroundin area.

As youngans we were always pretendin to be hunters, stalkin some wild animals or in search of Injuns.

We sat on the highest ground and climbed the tallest trees to look out to see what lay out yonder, past where we could see. It was our dream to someday explore those areas far away.

I worked for Charles Hoffman who owned Hoffman's Carriage Company in Gettysburg. As a tailor, it was my job to design and sew the harnesses for the carriages and buggies the company built. It was a good job for me cause I was a craftsman. I made sure each harness had my initials on it when it went out of the shop.

In the spring of 1856, Mr. Hoffman moved his company to Shepherdstown, Virginia. The carriages that he made already had a fine reputation in Virginia. His son John asked Edwin Skelly (my friend Jack's brother), my brother, William, John Snyder, Jerry Sheffler and myself, if we wanted to move there, to work at the new business. William said right away that he was stayin in Gettysburg.

I was 16 years old at the time. My parents let me make my own decision. I decided to go with the company to Virginia.

Part of my decision was that my salary would increase, with the added bonus of being able to share in the profits. If truth be known (and I am mostly a man who tells the truth), I moved for several other reasons. I thought it might be excitin to live by myself and not have to answer to anyone. And I wanted to get out from under the shadow of William. I was always compared to him.

If there had been no William to have to follow, I would have done just fine stayin in Gettysburg. In Virginia, I reckon no one ceptin Mr. Hoffman, his son, and my friends from Gettysburg who moved to Shepherdstown with me would know me. There would be no comparisons.

The four of us Gettysburg boys jumped at the chance to leave home and venture out on our own. I thought movin offered me great possibilities. I couldn't explain my reason for leavin to my mother and father or to my brother. They would have thought I was just jealous of William.

My parents didn't like my decision. They were sad to see me leave. Both of my sisters wished me well. When it was time to say good bye to William, he wasn't there. I thought that odd cause he was told when I was leavin.

The carriage company in Virginia was in a building on the corner of Princess Street and New Street in Shepherdstown. The brick building had a high dock in back where the buggies were set in the sun so the paint would dry. That dock was mighty high to me beins I was so short. The Hoffman family lived nearby.

The company had six workers besides the Hoffmans, including myself and Edwin Skelly, John Snyder and Jerry Shepler, all from Gettysburg and local Shepherdstown boys John Metz and Josiah Kitzmiller.

Shepherdstown was different than Gettysburg. It was much smaller with only one main street and with no diamond in its center. Where Gettysburg was mostly orchards and farmland, Shepherdstown was a river town, with businesses tied to the Chesapeake & Ohio Canal and the Potomac River. Shepherdstown had two flour mills, five churches, three schools, and two large hotels. It was said Shepherdstown had tried many years ago to become the country's capital. But it wasn't chosen.

Shepherdstown was a real old town, with a rich history going back to 1762. A huge stone tobacco warehouse sat on the shores of the Potomac River. Factories were busy, with machinery powered by the water from the town run.

Work was plentiful. We made carriages, buggies and all types of wagons. We repaired those made by other companies.

When I wasn't working, I boarded with John and Mary H. who had offered room and board to me as a worker at the carriage shop. They lived near the new Trinity Episcopal Church on German Street. I had one room. I paid monthly rent which included a small bedroom and an evenin meal that Mary prepared.

John and Mary were very friendly folk. I enjoyed my time with them.

I wrote often to let father and mother know how I was doin here and also to send them money to help them out.

There wasn't a day that went by that I didn't miss my mother and my sisters. As for my father and William, I don't remember thinkin about them at all. The thought of turnin back and goin home didn't appeal none to me either. I thought my future was here in this little town in Virginia.

In early November, 1856, a messenger had arrived at the shop with a telegram for me. I was quite happy to receive one, since I had never gotten one before. My happiness was short lived. The telegram was from my father, askin me to come home to Gettysburg. My mother had passed away unexpectedly. I was totally shocked.

I went home to attend the services. Everyone welcomed me ceptin for William. Our family all attended the funeral. I watched as mother was buried at Evergreen Cemetery. My sister, Annie, cooked a meal for all our friends and neighbors.

My friend, Jack Skelly, and I talked for several hours after the others left. He was gettin by real well in Gettysburg. I told him about my new job and with my life in Virginia.

Jack and his special girl, Jennie, were together and had talked about gettin married some day. To me that was a grand idea. It seemed like whenever Jack and I weren't together, the two of them were together. They were a good fit. I was hopin when they married they would raise lots of little ones. I was even hopin they would name one of their boys Wesley. I like Jennie about as well as any girl in Gettysburg.

When it was time to go back to Virginia, William grabbed me by the arm. I thought he was going to hit me. I stepped back. "She died because of you, ya know," he screamed.

"What are you talking about?" I yelled.

"Mother thought her little boy abandoned her by moving to Virginia. It made her very sad. She never got over it," he said.

"You take that back," I demanded, clenchin my fist and gettin ready to defend my honor.

"Never. I will never take it back, cause I am right. And you know it," he hollered, backin away from me.

Father arrived just in time to break up our fight. My brother ran off. My father put his hand on my shoulder. "Stay here in Gettysburg where your family is, Wesley. This is where you belong," he said in a sad tone of voice.

"I have a good job. I am gettin settled in at Shepherdstown," I explained, hopin he would understand. "I need to give it a little more time to see what I want to do."

"I respect your decision, even though I don't like it. God speed, my son. You know you can always come home."

"I know father. Good bye. And God bless." With that I began the trip back to Virginia.

Annie had written me after that apologizin for my brother's behavior. She said I was not at fault for my mother's death. In fact, mother had told her that she was happy I was out of the way so that William and my father would not bother me.

In 1859, I quit workin for the Hoffman Company and took a job in nearby Martinsburg, Virginia as a coach trimmer for Mr. John C. Allen. He offered me more money for doin the same job. Mr. Hoffman wished me well. He had no bad feelins about me leavin.

I continued to board with John and Mary on the weekends, but took a room at the Berkeley Hotel in Martinsburg. The hotel was owned by the Baltimore & Ohio Railroad.

Martinsburg was a railroad town. A large roundhouse was across the railroad tracks from the hotel. I watched the trains and all the activity goin on there from my front window on the third floor of the hotel.

Martinsburg was located exactly 100 miles from Baltimore. Martinsburg was where all the train crews had to switch cause they were only allowed to work for 100 miles.

The men all stayed at the Berkeley Hotel to wait for their next shift.

Business in Martinsburg was better cause it was a bigger town with more wagons to work on than when I was in Shepherdstown.

There was no better harness maker in the area than I was. My boss knew that and so did his customers. I liked the boys I worked with. Mr. Allen treated me right.

In late July, 1859, my sister told me that my father got married again to a woman half his age. I was not interested. I had a fine mother. She was gone. A step-mother did not fit into the future plans in my life. Annie invited me to come home for the weddin but didn't insist. She was on my side on this one and said she was only goin out of respect to father, not cause she was thrilled with the situation.

In mid-October, 1859, there was much excitement in Martinsburg. A group of outlaws attacked the federal arsenal at nearby Harpers Ferry. Volunteer militia, includin four units from Martinsburg, were called up to help end the raid. Many of those boys who were ordered to Harpers Ferry worked at the roundhouse.

The men who answered the call boarded the Baltimore and Ohio Railroad train near the hotel. Those men who left were from the Berkeley County Rifles, Rangers, Cavalry and Artillery.

Several days later, when the local boys returned, Lt. George Wollett, of the Martinsburg militia and a customer at Mr. Allen's shop, told us that his men were in the middle of a fierce fight. "We drove the raiders into a fire engine house and surrounded them. Marines came up from Washington to finish the job. Our local boys performed well. We suffered just a few wounded, with none killed in the action," the lieutenant boasted.

Another of our customers, David Hunter Strother, an artist and newspaper reporter for *Harpers Weekly*, was also on the scene of the events in Harpers Ferry. He told us that several thousand troops had gone there to capture the intruders. Strother's drawings of the incident appeared in the newspaper on November 5, 1859.

Strother's drawings and articles in *Harpers Weekly* followed the trial that resulted from the Harpers Ferry raid. One of the boys at the carriage shop read the newspaper to me. He said that the main leader of the raid was John Brown. Brown and six of his men were found guilty of treason, incitin slaves to rebel and murder. They were all hanged in Charlestown between the end of 1859 and the beginnin of 1860.

All the militia have now returned home with tales of watchin men hangin by the neck. It was not somethin I was interested in hearin about.

By summer of 1860, I was excited cause I was turnin twenty-one. Annie invited me to come home, promising a nice birthday party for me. I said no. I missed my sisters, but wasn't inclined to go back to Gettysburg again exceptin maybe in a year or two.

The presidential election in the fall of 1860 had everyone in this part of Virginia on edge. The locals were afraid that if Abraham Lincoln was elected, some states would secede from the Union. They said that civil war might follow.

The minute the results of the election were known and Lincoln was elected, there was even more talk of war. Mr. Lincoln didn't even get one vote in our part of the county. I had trouble figurin out how he won the election.

I wrote regular to Annie, sendin her a few dollars each time to help out. I knew she was raisin Julia by herself. She never told me nothin about father's new wife. Annie never said nothin bad about her cause we had been taught "if you can't say somethin nice, don't say nothin at all". I feared Annie would become an old maid takin care of Julia. There would be no time for Annie to do the proper courtin.

I had enlisted in the Hamtramck Guards, a Shepherdstown militia unit. All my friends were right there beside of me at the meetins and the trainin. The name seemed like a funny name for a guard unit of militia. But no one around

Shepherdstown thought the name was funny. One of their heroes from the Mexican War was Colonel Hamtramck. Our unit was named in his honor.

The militia met and talked of a possible war. We practiced marchin around town. We were mighty proud. So were the people of Shepherdstown. The ladies were quite happy that we were goin to be soldiers.

War talk was the excitement of the boys both in Martinsburg and Shepherdstown most days. When we were not talkin about other topics, we were talkin about makin war.

To the boys here, their loyalty was not questioned. They were joinin up to protect their land from those Yanks who would gladly come here and take everythin away from us.

Most around here knew I was a Yankee by birth, havin grown up in Pennsylvania. Lately I wasn't feelin real connected to any of the Pennsylvania boys, exceptin maybe those friends and neighbors from Gettysburg. I could not imagine why those boys back home would take up arms to fuss about the secession of some southern states, cause from what I had been told, it was all legal and proper.

I knew a lot more about bein a harness maker than bein a soldier or about secession arguments. I left that to the smarter boys. But even for a little fellow, I was a pretty good fighter. The idea of takin on some enemy soldiers was appealin to me.

In my family, I often had to fight for my rights. I have been in a few good scrapes in my day and have won my share.

I am just a wee fellow – only about five feet tall even standing on my tip toes. But do not let my smallness make you think I ain't tough. I am, in fact, tough as nails and probably the toughest little man anyone around here has ever seen. But the toughness does not ever show less I am excited.

Bein small sometimes was an advantage, cause the other boys did not give me credit for bein a fighter. They thought I would run when the goin got tough. That usually allowed me to get the first couple of licks in when they were not expectin them. Runnin -- oh, I could do that too. If the fightin wasn't workin out, I could run from the fastest of them.

On April 12, 1861, Fort Sumter, somewhere in South Carolina, was shelled. Within a few days the federal fort surrendered to those South Carolina boys. The new President, Mr. Lincoln, called out troops to fight for the Union.

I had told Annie in my letter that if a war started, I was goin to stay here and enlist in Virginia. Annie's letter said my brother William had comments about that. She said his kinder comment was that I was a traitor. She said his other thoughts were not worth printin in her letter.

I was not surprised that William didn't care of my decision to enlist here in Virginia.

Our boys didn't have to wait long cause Virginia officially voted at the convention to leave the Union on April 17. We were told to be prepared to leave when we got the call. My boss, Mr. Allen, accepted the news that I was joinin up. He wished me well.

On April 20, I got the message in Martinsburg. I dropped everythin and hitched a ride in a buggy from one of our customers to Shepherdstown. I was one of the last to run to the center of town to line up and be counted. The rest of my friends were already in line. We were ready and rarin to go. Nothin could have calmed me as that was the most excitin day of my life.

We lined up, just as we had practiced. We were a determined bunch who wanted to prove that the people of the Commonwealth of Virginia had no fears while we were protectin them. The orders came to proceed. We marched through the streets of Shepherdstown.

The people from town stood along the streets and cheered. We doffed our caps in a return salute, as we marched toward Kearneysville and to the train that would take us to the recruiting station at Harpers Ferry.

I wondered what was in store for us. Everyone talked about a short war. We would be enlistin for a short time. We thought it could not be that bad. Our lads were eager and ready. We expected life to be much more excitin than it was on a regular day in Shepherdstown or Martinsburg.

I had joined the militia as a way to meet others my own age. Those boys I had met through that militia unit were now marchin beside me.

As we marched, I took a look down the line. Marching next to me was John, my closest friend in Shepherdstown. He and I spent a lot of time together when I was not workin. I liked Mary, John's wife, even better than I liked John, but I did not let him know that. I don't think John would have understood.

Marchin further down in the line was John Snyder and Jerry Sheffler, also from Gettysburg and men who had worked at the Hoffman Carriage shop with me. They were still my friends, havin no bad feelins that I took a job at another shop. Others directly around me today were T. Harris Towner (the postmaster), Daniel Morgan Entler and Benjamin Pendleton, all men I had known for several years.

Missin, and not marchin with us was my friend Edwin Skelly, who had worked for the Hoffman Carriage shop as a carriage painter. Edwin had returned to Gettysburg.

Edwin and I had talked about the decision we each had to make. Edwin also had family back in Gettysburg, including his brother (my best friend, Jack Skelly), their mother and father, his younger brother, Daniel and his two sisters.

"You have friends here. You seem to be at home in Virginia," Edwin told me. "But for me, Gettysburg is home. I belong there. I'm going to help my family at home."

"I'm stayin, Edwin. My family ain't gonna like it none, but I am goin to help Virginia," I told him. "You are right. This feels like home to me. You take care, Edwin. And keep an eye out for your brother, Jack. Tell him to keep his head down and be safe."

We joked about how the soldiers I was enlistin with might someday meet up with the Gettysburg boys. I was not havin good thoughts about havin to shoot at my friends from Gettysburg.

We agreed it was goin to be a big war and we would go our separate ways. I promised to return to Gettysburg for a visit after the war where we could compare our stories. We shook hands and wished each other well. And then he left to return to Gettysburg instead of enlistin with me.

I had no bad feelins about Edwin goin back to Gettysburg. It was his decision to make. He made it. I made mine.

Several others from Shepherdstown decided to take their horses and join the 1st Virginia Cavalry. Those included William A. Morgan, Dr. Isaac Tanner, William Henry Hagan, Redmond Burke and his three sons, Frank, John and Mathew Burke.

All of us from the Hamtramck Guards were goin to enlist to protect our land from the northern invasion we were told would start happenin any day now. Up to that time, we had just been pretendin to be soldiers. Today we were enlistin. The pretendin was over. We were goin to be real soldiers someday soon.

When the train arrived, we climbed aboard for the short ride to Harpers Ferry. As the train bumped down the rails, the boys talked about stickin together like glue. Each of us pledged to look out for each other. Hopefully that would get us all home alive soon.

At Harpers Ferry, we all stood in line for what seemed like hours, to sign the papers.

For me, it did not go quite as well at the recruitin station as I thought it would. When I got to the front of the line, the recruiter took one look at me and said, "Come back in a few years when you are old enough." And then he motioned for me to step out of the way of the others.

I wanted to put up a fight, but I knew cause I was so short, I looked real young, even though most 13 year olds did not have a beard like I had. In fact, I was 21 years old and older than many of the Hamtramck Guards.

I knew there was nothin I could tell the man that would change his mind. I decided to go to find John Hoffman, owner of the Hoffman Carriage shop, to ask him for help. He had known me all my life and had marched with us today to help us get settled. And he offered to go back in line to help me.

This time when it was my turn, the recruiter looked up. He started in on me again. I held up my hand. Mr. Hoffman stepped forward. "Sir, I am a well-respected businessman from Shepherdstown. I have known this man as John Wesley Culp all my life. In spite of his size and appearance, I will swear by my oath and signature, that he was born in 1839," Mr. Hoffman said.

The recruiter looked me up and down and shook his head. "It is hard to believe this boy's old enough to enlist," he suggested, "but I will take your oath and signature that he is of proper age. I will allow him to enlist."

He pushed papers forward that Mr. Hoffman signed. I thanked Mr. Hoffman and promised him I would owe him. And then, just when I thought my worries were over, I was given my musket. We were issued Harpers Ferry made regular army percussion muskets with a bayonet. When I placed the musket on my shoulder to aim, my finger did not reach the trigger. The stock was too long.

Mr. Hoffman came to my rescue again. He took the musket. When he returned, he had cut several inches off the musket stock so my finger could reach the trigger.

We wore our Hamtramck Guards uniforms issued to us over a year ago. Others just got new uniforms today. My bein a tailor paid off. I made some extra money alterin uniforms for many of the other boys.

We were issued a bedroll and ammunition. That first night in camp I took out my knife and whittled "W. Culp" in the musket's stock. It was not really necessary. No other rebel soldier could use it cause his arm would have been too long. The carvin was for me. I made sure everyone knew this musket was mine.

None of us Shepherdstown lads slept much that first night. We were too excited. We wanted to start fightin them Yanks tomorrow mornin. We yapped about it all night.

14

Of course, the next mornin there were no enemy sol-diers in sight. But lookin in every direction, there were lots of us Virginians. We were proud and eager.

We were set in lines and inspected. Not a one of us looked real promisin as a soldier. But the officer in charge told us by the time he got done marchin and drillin us, we would be as good as any army that had ever marched.

J. Wesley Culp
NPS photo

Early 1861
William Esaias Culp

My name is William Esaias Culp. My friends mostly call me William. I got the Esaias part from my father, Esaias Jesse Culp. I don't know anyone else in the world besides him and me who have that particular name. I was born in Petersburg, Pennsylvania on August 8, 1831.

I am 29 years old. I live in Gettysburg, Pennsylvania with my father and mother and two sisters. I have a little brother, Wesley, who lives somewhere in Virginia. I am trained as a coach trimmer.

As the oldest son in our family, I considered it my duty to work hard and become a leader. And to set a good example for my brother and sisters.

My job had been with the Hoffman Carriage Company of Gettysburg, makers of fine buggies and carriages. About five years ago, they moved their company to Virginia. My brother Wesley and several of my neighbors moved with the company. I chose to stay in Gettysburg. I now do coach trimming for several businesses here.

In November, 1856, mother had become quite ill and died. My father sent a telegram to my brother, Wesley, informing him of her death. When he came home, I confronted Wesley, blaming his leaving on mother's passing. After all, he was her prize baby. He had abandoned her by moving south. The incident turned ugly.

I had decided that with a war looming on the horizon, I would proudly take up arms to keep the Union together. We had received Wesley's letter recently explaining that he was enlisting – but his enlistment would be in the southern army and was a way for him to protect his new homeland in Virginia. He was a traitor in my eyes. I don't know what he thought he was protecting Virginia from. Virginia and the other states had seceded illegally.

Recently we had welcomed Edwin Skelly back home. He was a Gettysburg boy who had moved with Wesley to Virginia. Edwin was a tad smarter than my brother and was doing the right thing. Edwin's brother, Jack, and I quizzed Edwin when he arrived.

"Why didn't Wesley come back home?" I asked.

"Said he was home there," Edwin announced. "Seems like he's more like them now than like us."

"We ain't waiting no more," I said, turning to Jack, Wesley's best friend. "We're joining up without him."

"I don't like it," Jack said. "But he made his bed. Now he must lay in it."

Edwin tried to convince me later that Wesley's decision was a good one for him personally. I wasn't buying it. I wasn't even going to listen to the dribble that he was spewing on Wesley's behalf.

"*Damn you, Wesley*," I cursed to myself. "*Wasn't ever a day you did anything right, boy. If I ever come across you on the field, I will not hesitate to put a ball right between your eyes. Of course, I'd deny it if anyone asked. But a man's gotta do what a man's gotta do. And brother or no brother, you are now the enemy.*"

In recent times my friends around town talked often about what was happening with the southern states leaving the country right and left following the secession of South Carolina. Us Pennsylvania lads wanted to do our part to help hold the Union together.

The Independent Blue Militia Company, a band of seventy or so friends and neighbors from here in Gettysburg and Adams County, had been formed for a long time. Many of us had joined several years ago just to be together. We practiced marching as best we could, getting our information from military manuals.

As the war loomed on the horizon, our activities became more and more focused. Our lads were very eager. We just did not have a very good idea of how to train for

18

whatever we would soon be facing. Our company really needed someone to teach us the proper ways. And the sooner that happened, the sooner we would be ready to step into the action.

I read all the newspapers I could get my hands on to find out what was happening in the country. I read that Governor Curtin of Pennsylvania was determined to provide soldiers to support our new President, Abraham Lincoln. The newspapers reported that those wanting to hold the Union together and those wanting to leave the country were headed on a collision course. The country was likely heading toward war.

If and when that happened, the Independent Blue Militia Company had already voted to be among the first to step forward to enlist.

My father and I talked about what my role would be. Father said he would be proud to see me march to war for our country. He thought I would make a good officer, particularly because I was a little older and more mature than many of the other area boys.

My decision to sign up was probably a bit more difficult than my friends' decisions because I had to leave my wife, Salmone. We were married in 1853. Salmone was unhappy about my decision but she was understanding. We talked about the duty of the Gettysburg boys to go together and be a part of the war efforts to save our country.

I reminded her that we were only going to sign up for ninety days.

With the bombardment of Fort Sumter, all bets were off. The war had begun.

I assured Salmone that with President Lincoln's call up of seventy-five thousand soldiers, we would bring the states who left the Union back by the end of three months.

I was sure our local boys would make President Lincoln happy to have us on his side. After all, Pennsylvania played an important part in the Revolutionary War. We wanted to keep up the tradition of the Keystone State. Many of the boys signed up with the promise that we would be "home guards". They would be paid as soldiers but would see no action in the war. That didn't appeal to me. I wanted to fight to end this rebellion and to bring the Union together for President Lincoln.

The boys from the Independent Blue Militia Company offered our services to Governor Curtin. He graciously accepted our seventy-five men.

I strutted proudly down the street with all the volunteers. The town's people cheered us. Women waved handkerchiefs as we passed by. We were ready to save the Union for President Lincoln, all by ourselves.

We were mustered into Company E, the 2nd Pennsylvania Volunteers. Among our boys enlisting together on April 29, 1861 were myself, Captain Charles H. Buehler, our leader, Johnston H. "Jack" Skelly, Jr., Theodore Norris, Nicholas J. Codori, the Sheads brothers (John and Isaac), William F. Weikert, Peter Warren, George "Temp" Little, William H. Little, Duncan Little, John T. McIlhenny, William McGonigal, Franklin Duphorn, J. Louis McClellan, Adam Doerson, Jr., Edward Fahnestock, Peter Warren, John Arendt and his sons John Jr. and George, and others.

John and Isaac Sheads were Salmone's brothers, and therefore my brothers-in-law. All told there were seventy five boys from Gettysburg who enlisted in the 2nd Pennsylvania Volunteers that day.

We were sent for training at York, Pennsylvania. We waited several hours for the train to Hanover Junction. We were crammed into the cars. There was no getting a nap in on the way as the train rumbled noisily along the rickety rails. When we finally arrived a few hours later, we were cheered like heroes by the people at the train station.

The 1st, 2nd and 3rd Pennsylvania Volunteers were all together. Those three units were made up of boys from Allentown, Easton, Reading, Gettysburg, Harrisburg, Lancaster, Chambersburg, Columbia, West Chester, Altoona, Bloomfield, Hollidaysburg, Johnstown and various other Pennsylvania towns.

At age 29, there were a few men in our little army who were older than I was. Perhaps a dozen were upwards of 35 to 40 years old. But mostly our regiment was made up of real young boys. Our youngest, a drummer boy named Wallace Ziegler, who wasn't officially part of us but ran off and followed us everywhere, I doubt was older than twelve.

William Esaias Culp
Adams County Historical Society
Gettysburg, Pennsylvania

Early 1861
Johnston Hastings "Jack" Skelly Jr.

My name is Johnston Hastings Skelly Jr. I was born in Gettysburg on August 4, 1841. My friends all call me "Jack." I imagine that was so no one confused me with my father, Johnston Hastings Skelly Sr. I am the younger brother of Charles Edwin who we call Edwin, the older brother of Daniel and the best friend of Wesley Culp. I have two sisters, Anne and Sallie. My mother, father, brothers and sisters and I live on West Middle Street in Gettysburg. Unlike my father and brother who were in the carriage business, I was a stone mason by trade.

If ever I had a confusing day in my life, it was today. It wasn't cause I was unsure about joining up. No siree. I was real sure I was going to help the cause of Abraham Lincoln, our new President, to save the Union. I thought the secesh rebellion had to be crushed.

I was delighted to see my friends and neighbors enlisting right beside me. And I was happier than a hog wallowing in the mud that my brother Edwin had returned home from Virginia to be with the family. Edwin and I were pretty close. I had missed him being around in the years he had been in Virginia working. He was a tailor and had left to work in Virginia alongside my friend, Wesley Culp, in the mid-1850s.

Two things were troubling to me personally. First, my best friend in the world, Wesley Culp, had chosen to stay in Virginia and was joining the rebel army. That made him my enemy. And that was very hard for me to understand and accept. I couldn't for the life of me picture my friend in an enemy uniform. And I certainly couldn't think about shooting at him or trying to kill him, even though he was the enemy.

Growing up together, Wesley Culp and I played almost every day. In school we sat next to each other. We helped each other with the lessons. We competed against each other on a daily basis and worked on various projects together. If there was mischief to be found, we were together in that too.

On days where there was no school, we were exploring the hills and fields all around the borough of Gettysburg. We knew all the interesting places to hide out.

When we played, I followed Wesley just about anywhere. Each day he would lead me to a new place. Each one was a little further away than the place we had gone the day before.

There was a wide area around Gettysburg where we fished, hunted, swam and hiked. We knew every hill and every place that a young boy could hide. We were always on the move. We were constantly plotting our next adventure. Cause Wesley was merely five feet tall, I was there to give him a boost – onto a tall rock or up a tree. But in spite of his size, he was pound-for-pound the toughest lad I knew. Several boys at school pushed him too far and ended up on the ground, not willing to try him again anytime soon.

Wesley and I knew every person who lived in the area. We knew which ones were most likely to allow us to explore their lands. Sometimes when we didn't think we would be allowed, we would explore it without permission and hope we would be fast enough to avoid trouble if we were discovered some place where we didn't belong.

Wesley was the leader. I was the follower.

My second concern was that I was marching away from my best girl, Jennie, and my mother. They were the two most important ladies in my life. Depending on what day it was determined who was more important of the two at that specific time. I was not sure I could survive even a day without them. And now I was marching off for at least three months.

My troubles weren't cause I was a baby -- cause believe me, I ain't a baby. I am a man who is nearly 20 years old. It was just that when a man is close to his mother and his girlfriend, he doesn't want to leave them alone cause they might be too upset to carry on for themselves. They needed me lots more than I needed them. At least that's what they told me.

When it came time for my decision to go to war, I gave it hardly a thought. I was going to fight for my country.

I did, however, want to tell Jennie and my mother that I was enlisting.

Jennie and I had been lifelong friends. Her father, James Wade, had been an apprentice to my father's tailor shop for three years by the time I was born. Mr. Wade was a frequent visitor to our house when I was just a youngan. I liked Mr. Wade all right though it seemed like he was always in trouble with the local constable. I liked his daughter even more.

When I finally told Jennie that I was enlisting, she was not happy at all that I was going to war. In fact, she cried and cried. I tried to get her to understand.

I explained that "Mr. Lincoln needs all of us Gettysburg boys to help restore the Union and bring it back together." And I believed that in my heart. The more arguments I made, telling her that I was needed more in the war than in Gettysburg, the more she cried.

I promised her I would write her on a regular basis wherever I was. And I would be careful so that I would not be a war casualty. She agreed to write to me too.

Jennie and I had recently talked seriously about getting married. We would live in Gettysburg, buy a farm and raise lots of children. We didn't tell anyone in either family about that. They were already upset just cause I was leaving.

Jennie wrapped her arms around me just before I left. It felt like she didn't want to let go. She told me she would miss me. And she said she would faithfully write to me.

When I left Jennie's house, I met with my mother. I told her "My country needs me." And then I asked, "May I go?" She held me tight and then followed Jennie's lead. She cried and cried. "Yes, my boy," she said proudly stopping just long enough to answer. "And may God bless and keep you." And then she cried for a while longer.

While mother was upset that we were going off to war, my father was mighty proud.

My brothers, Daniel and Edwin, were upset that I was enlisting. I told them that they had a responsibility here in Gettysburg to help mother and father get by without their oldest brother being around. My chores were split between the two of them. They didn't want to hear any of that.

My two sisters cried – but aren't little girls supposed to cry in situations like that? There was no trying to explain the importance of my enlistment to them. The fact that their oldest brother was going to war made it hard enough on them.

I enlisted for three months in Company E, the 2nd Pennsylvania Infantry on April 29, 1861 in Gettysburg. Wesley's brother, William Culp, and seventy three other boys from Gettysburg joined with me.

Johnston Hastings "Jack" Skelly, Jr.
From the John White Johnston Collection
Rochester Museum and Science Center
Rochester, New York

Early 1861
Mary Virginia Wade

My name is Mary Virginia Wade. I was born in Gettysburg, Pennsylvania on May 21, 1843. My parents are James Wade, Sr. and Mary Ann Filby Wade. I have an older sister, Georgia, and three younger brothers, John James (known to us as Jack), Samuel and Henry. We lived on Baltimore Street in Gettysburg in a house that also served as my father's tailor shop.

I am called by several names, depending who is calling. On those rare occasions my mother is angry, I am "Mary Virginia Wade." At many other times, my friends have called me "Ginnie", "Gen", and "Jennie." I answer to all those names on any given day.

It has been two days since the boys from Gettysburg have marched off to enlist in the Union Army. I was proud as peaches. Over seventy boys have left Gettysburg to help save the Union. I understood President Lincoln needed them more than we did. But I was also afraid.

As I watched them march through the streets on their way to enlist, I felt all mixed up. I was proud to know many of them and excited that they were willing to fight for the Union cause. I knew that Pennsylvania, being such a large state, must do its part to save the Union. But their enlisting conflicted with my fears for their well being. I wondered who would come back and who would not.

When my Gettysburg neighbors and friends discussed their decision to join the army, my family understood. We were supportive. With all that understanding and support, however, I personally was torn when my life-long friend and sweetheart, Jack Skelly, told me he was enlisting too.

Jack was more special than all the others. We had been partners and best friends all our lives. He talked to me for a long time and convinced me that our country needed him and the Gettysburg boys. He said the town could get along without them for the ninety days it would take to end the war.

I was selfish in thinking he should not go. I was worried that when he left he would forget he had a girlfriend back home. I could not stand that thought. I did not want this war getting in the way of our relationship even for a short period of time. But then I decided that surely I could make it for ninety days without feeling his arms wrapped around me.

Jack had been real upset that his best friend, Wesley Culp, had taken up with the enemy. I told Jack that he shouldn't worry, cause the chances in a big war of fighting against Wesley's unit was quite unlikely.

Jack seemed confused that Wesley had joined the other side. Maybe he took it personally that Wesley didn't come home. I know the Culp family. I am thinking that Wesley's decision had more to do with his good-for-nothing brother, William Esaias, than it had to do with anything else.

I knew from Wesley's mother, God rest her soul, that Wesley was often left out in family matters. Wesley felt that William never accepted him. She told me that Wesley's father and brother often ganged up on him and left him out of activities they shared only with each other. His father and brother were alike – stubborn and righteous. Wesley was much more level-headed and likeable. No wonder he preferred living in Virginia. I didn't blame Wesley for trying to get out from under his brother's shadow.

I did worry about some of the other Gettysburg lads. Of course, I didn't personally know more than a handful myself. Some seemed real young to serve. My own brothers, Jack, Samuel, and Henry, were too young. Thank the good Lord for that.

My older sister, Georgia, was engaged to Louis J. McClellan, one of the lads who marched off and joined up. Georgia was even more worried than I was. I was certain that when I am not fretting about Jack and the others, I would have to look after her too.

I was also concerned because all the "men of the house" had enlisted together. I should explain. My father had been in jail for some years now. Even on the rare occasions that he was out, although I loved him, I refused to see him. My mother had banned my father for visiting our house. She had more than enough of his shenanigans. So you see, Jack, has been the kind of "man of the house" -- sharing the load with Louis McClellan.

I promised to write to Jack. I promised my mother that I would continue to sew for her and the other Gettysburg ladies. I promised Georgia that I would comfort her in Louis' absence. I don't know when I will have time to worry about the other Gettysburg lads with all the pledges I have already made.

Mary Virginia Wade
Adams County Historical Society
Gettysburg, Pennsylvania

Part II

Spring 1861
John Wesley Culp

The members of the Hamtramck Guards were assigned to Company B, 2nd Virginia Volunteer Infantry, commanded by Colonel James W. Allen. We were told that Colonel Allen was a good officer, a recent graduate of the Virginia Military Institute and was trained in military tactics.

Our camp was set up on Bolivar Heights, which was just above the town of Harpers Ferry, Virginia.

Colonel Allen addressed our regiment. He was short and to the point. "Today you are playing the game of pretending to be a soldier. Soon I am going to make you into real soldiers. For most of you that will not come easily. I hope you are up to the task," the Colonel screamed. To prove that he was tryin to make soldiers out of us, he drilled us from mornin to night, every single day.

We proved Colonel Allen right. We did not look like soldiers or act like soldiers. We looked like farmers and harness makers and shop keepers cause that was what we were. We marched in crooked lines. We each marched to our own master.

If Colonel Allen was to make soldiers out of us, it would take some doin on his part. We were certainly eager and willin. But there was a long distance between wantin to be good soldiers and what we were up to this point.

Colonel Allen's ways were simple enough. We marched and drilled in the mornin. We marched and drilled some more in the afternoon. And then we marched and drilled in the evenin. And the next day we started out to do it all over again. Someone in Company C who had a time piece figured we drilled 12 hours every day.

If we weren't drillin, we were just marchin. I hated to march and I hated to drill. The marchin made me so tired I could barely put one foot in front of the other. It became automatic. I think at times I was marchin in my sleep.

My feet hurt every minute of every day. My blisters never healed. My shoes were not made for marchin. My little feet were not a good fit in my shoes even when I was just sittin under a tree.

When it rained, I took off my shoes and socks and put them in my knapsack to keep them dry. The mud soothed my sore feet until I stepped on somethin sharp. That made them hurt even worse.

Because of the length of my legs, I was not able to march in step with the other men. It wasn't cause I was stupid. For me it was not possible cause I took shorter steps. I had to take more steps than the boys on either side of me. After bein called out of line and yelled at several times for marchin out of step, I think Colonel Allen finally realized I was not goin to improve. Or perhaps it was some of the Hamtramck Guards askin him to really take a look at my step, measurin it and then determinin that I actually could not keep up. After all, I had the shortest legs in the whole regiment. Yellin at me was not likely to make my legs grow longer. I think Colonel Allen liked my spirit and persistence. I was tryin to keep up. Perhaps that's why he did not send me home.

When we did the double quick, I had to step out of line to keep from gettin run over by the boys behind me.

Actually I wasn't the only one who was real small in my regiment. I met two others who was just five feet tall too. They was George Colbert of Company G and James Blamer of Company E. We sat together one night to discuss how little soldiers with big hearts could help our boys win the war.

In the beginnin, I thought the drillin was a waste of time. First the officers had to teach some of the men their right from their left. I do not know how many times men crashed together when the command "right face" was given, as about as many men turned left as right. If battles were to be won or lost from field commands, our men were doomed.

Our officers taught us the manual of arms which was a nine-step drill to shoot our muskets. You couldn't shoot if you didn't go through the steps in the proper order. We did the drill over and over and over and over. Even after all that drillin, some of the boys still got mixed up with the countin. I did not think any amount of drillin was goin to make soldiers out of this bunch of misfits.

The only part we could be sure of every day besides drillin and marchin was pails of coffee. From the time the bugle call raised the troops in the mornin until we fell into our tents at the end of the day, coffee was what kept us goin. On days we had brown sugar, the coffee was even better.

At the end of April, the Governor sent us a new officer, Colonel Thomas J. Jackson. Within four weeks, another officer, Brigadier General Joseph Johnston took over the whole division of men. Our 2nd Virginia boys were assigned to part of a new brigade under command of Colonel Jackson, along with the 5th, 27th and 33rd Virginia boys.

I thought about my sisters Annie and Julia but couldn't get out no mail to Gettysburg cause of the war.

I worried about Annie and the burdens that my mother's death had left for her. When father married again, Julia and her were not ready to have a step mother. Our mother had just been gone for three years. They knew father was lonely but they preferred to take one day at a time and try to make it on their own without a stranger movin into the house and orderin them around. I was happy that I was not in Gettyburg.

Annie was right about a lot of things. Her letters have been a comfort to me. It was goin to be hard for me to get by without getting letters from Annie.

In early June, a telegram was waitin for me when we got back to camp. It contained sad news. My father had died.

I was shocked. Annie, who sent the telegram, said my duty was to come home to the funeral.

I disagreed. I thought my duty was here. I was saddened that my father had died. But all I could do was pray for his soul while I was at camp here. I was not goin to return to Gettysburg. I did not feel close to my father. William was his favorite. I was not. I sat alone under a tree and tried to think of a time when my father had supported me. I could think of none.

I thought of my father only as a man who worked real hard and real long hours. When he was home he did not talk much. I did not know him well at all. I was not even sure that I ever liked him.

He took William fishin and huntin. They spent lots of time together. I do not know why, but father never took me anywhere. Seemed to me that father was on the same side with William.

Mother had tried to explain to me that William and my father meant no harm. They loved me in their own way. I really did not believe that, even comin from mother. Their actions spoke loudly to me. Neither of them liked havin me around.

I said a prayer, thankin God that my father went quickly. And that he would soon be united with my mother. That was how I paid my respects from camp in my own way.

I sent a telegram back to my sisters from the telegraph office in Harpers Ferry sayin I could not get a pass to come home. That wasn't really true, but I wanted to give her an excuse to answer whoever asked. I hadn't asked for a pass cause I was not interested in goin to the funeral.

In camp I was introduced to Henry Kyd Douglas, also a member of the Hamtramck Guards. He was mustered in two days before us at Halltown. He bragged that he would be home two days before our enlistments were up. And he was more than likely right on that account.

Douglas was a lawyer from Franklin and Marshall College and some famous law school. Douglas said he had studied the United States Constitution in class. He was certain that states had a right to secede if they wanted to. And he had joined the Confederate Army cause of those beliefs.

Douglas said he lived in a large brick house called Ferry Hill Place, kind of lookin down the river high above the Chesapeake and Ohio canal, on the Maryland side of the Potomac River across from Shepherdstown. It was located just a few hundred yards across the Potomac River from Virginia, now a Southern state. His mother had died when he was young. His father had remarried and the family had moved into his step-mother's house at Ferry Hill.

For weeks on end, we marched back and forth, between Martinsburg and Winchester and all the towns in between. We camped in six or seven different places on the way.

The men in the camps complained. One man from Company I said that Colonel Jackson "was killin up their sons by hard and useless marchin." Some called the colonel crazy for marchin us so hard and mostly to nowhere in particular.

On June 14, Colonel Jackson received orders for us to abandon camp at Bolivar Heights, Virginia. General Johnston had told our officers that the ground could not easily be defended. We were anxious to go up against some Yanks and to see if the drills had made soldiers of us. We were excited that perhaps this meant we were finally goin to join the war.

Various companies were sent out to destroy all bridges on the Potomac River between Point of Rocks in Maryland and Shepherdstown. The boys in Company B got orders to march to Shepherdstown and to destroy the covered bridge across the Potomac River. The bridge was an important link between Maryland and Virginia. That link needed to be broken. It was our job to set fire to the bridge.

The boys of Company B, now part of the First Brigade, marched to Shepherdstown in the dark. The orders were given. Douglas and I were two of the torch bearers for the burnin of the bridge.

Douglas told me his doubts about of our unit's first important assignment. He certainly would obey the orders. But his father, Reverend Robert Douglas, was a stockholder in the bridge company. Douglas said the bridge had been built around 1849 when it replaced Blackford's ferry. He was not real excited about havin to destroy the bridge partially owned by his father. We lined the entire bridge with dry straw, making our job pretty easy. We torched the straw and within minutes the whole bridge was ablaze. People from all over the area, on both sides of the river, watched it burn. Some cheered. Others did not seem happy with our mission. We watched as the timbers of the bridge fell into the river. I knew now the only place left to cross the river was downstream about a mile at Blackford's Ford.

As the bridge burned, Douglas said "I realize that war has begun." If there was ever someone to say that you should not burn your bridges behind you, it would be Douglas. He had just burned his father's bridge behind him.

Douglas also figured that from that point forward, there was no turning back. Right or wrong, our families were not only on the other side of the bridge, but on the other side of the war. Even if the bridge here was ever rebuilt, we were not real sure that the split in our families could be as easily mended.

After we burned the bridge in Shepherdstown, we marched to Martinsburg and then north to Camp Stephens near Hoke's Run. We were told to sleep on our arms as the federal army was expected to cross the river just north of us at Williamsport, Maryland and into Virginia any day now.

Our camp contained almost three thousand men, from the 2nd Virginia, the 4th Virginia and 5th Virginia, the 1st Virginia Cavalry, and the 1st Rockbridge Artillery. When we arrived, instead of fightin, we continued to drill. We drilled once after the sun came up, once from 11 until noon, and then three times in the afternoon and evening. At least we weren't doin any long marches.

Company B had no tents and slept on the ground. Some of the other boys had received new tents they had just gotten.

Several companies marched to Martinsburg to help Colonel Jackson burn some railroad property belongin to the Baltimore and Ohio Railroad at the roundhouse. It was the roundhouse that was right across the street from my room at the Berkeley Hotel. The railroad was a Yankee railroad vital to their supply lines that had to be destroyed. The companies in charge of the destruction came back with stories of a burnin inferno in Martinsburg. We could see and smell the smoke from camp.

Our boys talked about a possible battle. None of us even knew where the war was. We were tired of marchin and drillin. We wanted to find us some Yankees to shoot. Were we ready to fight if ordered to? We really did not know the answer to that question.

Henry Kyd Douglas

Spring 1861
William Esaias Culp

When we arrived at Hanover Junction we were trans-
ferred to the Northern Central Railroad to travel to
Baltimore, Maryland. Our orders got changed enroute.
Instead, we were brought back and taken to the fairgrounds
in York, Pennsylvania where we set up our encampment at
Camp Scott.

The place was named after the leader of the United
States Army, General Winfield Scott. There were about
5,500 soldiers in our camp. We were assigned sleeping
quarters on the straw inside the sheds at the fairgrounds. The
sheds had been the home of cattle before we got there. We
could still smell that they had recently been here.

General Robert Patterson was in command. The Gettysburg boys were assigned to his division. Our regimental
commander was Colonel Frederick S. Stambaugh.

I was not sure old General Patterson was spry enough to
handle the assignment of leading the young Union boys of
the Second Division. The old and crusty general was perhaps
70. He was said to have been a veteran of both the War of
1812 and the Mexican War. But I was certain he had the
training and experience that would help us succeed as
soldiers.

I will give General Patterson one thing. He was certainly in favor of marching and drilling our boys. In the first
few weeks, it was said we marched upwards of 150 miles.
And through all that, we never once got more than thirty-five
miles from York. And General Patterson never gave us even
ten minutes of warning to get prepared to do whatever the
orders were. When he gave the order, we moved out right
away.

I was not sure, however, if large amounts of drilling would produce brave soldiers. The more we drilled, the more I wondered.

All of us Gettysburg boys in Company E were under the command of Captain Charles H. Buehler. We all knew him. He had been the town burgess back in Gettysburg. He was real well liked by most of us.

Some of the Pennsylvania boys were sent to guard the railroad lines between here and the state line in Maryland. Company E was not among them.

We were sure we'd be safe and out of the way of any harm here in York. We had not heard of any rebel soldiers in Maryland or Pennsylvania. But we weren't real sure we were helping President Lincoln much either. Basically some of us wanted to shoot at some southern boys of the traitorous rebel army.

When Captain Buehler complained of our crooked lines, someone in the back yelled out "Captain you can grow more corn in crooked rows than in straight ones."

After a few weeks, we were bored and tired of marching and we were no nearer the war than we had been before we enlisted. Several men suggested we should all desert. The next morning we got a reminder from General Patterson of what happened to deserters when they were caught. They were shot by a firing squad. Most of us choose not to desert and risk getting caught.

I wrote regularly to my dear wife, Salmone. I wanted her to know how much I missed her already. I wanted her to know that I was safe at camp with no enemy nearby. I told her we regularly had visitors from Gettysburg. If she needed to send me anything, she could latch on to one of those neighbors who were coming by. I promised to send money to her, but we had not been paid.

Our boys had been issued old Harpers Ferry muskets, converted from flintlock to percussion. We lined up early and often to practice the manual of arms, by the numbers drill. Officers instructed our company in the precise movements required to load and fire a musket. Those instructions included nine steps we had to learn, memorize and be so comfortable with that we could load our muskets and fire them in our sleep. But that wasn't the purpose of the exercise. The purpose was to make us so familiar with the technique that we could fire the weapon in the heat of the battle. We needed to be able to load calmly even with someone charging at us with a bayonet and shoot them dead before they pushed their deadly bayonet into us. It was us or them.

So we learned to 1) reach into our cartridge pouch and pull out a paper encased cartridge consisting of a powder charge and ball, 2) place the paper cartridge in our teeth and tear the paper open, 3) empty the powder into the musket barrel and insert the ball, 4) draw the ram rod out of its sheath under the musket barrel, 5) ram the powder and ball into the barrel, 6) return the ram rod to its former position under the barrel, 7) cock the hammer and place the percussion cap, 8) aim, and 9) pull the trigger to fire the weapon. And then start all over again.

It got so I could fire my musket three times within a minute. Others were much slower. I was hoping the speed I was able to fire my weapon would buy me time and save my life. I certainly did not want to be a casualty of this war, even though I knew that was a possibility well beyond my control.

I could not even think of this war making my wife, Salmone, a widow. Boys not married could die, but dieing wasn't an option for me.

We drilled at 9, 10, 2 and 6 each day. I was not sure the drilling would make us good soldiers.

When we weren't marching or drilling, I spent my time practicing firing my musket on the range. Simple targets had been set up outside of camp.

I had always hunted and was a pretty good shot. I was lucky, I had a rifled bore that was more accurate than some of the smooth bore muskets the rest of my friends carried. With those guns it was hard to hit anyone unless he was real darn close. I had read that the army had tested the .69 caliber smooth bore musket in 1860 and found that it was 74%

accurate at 100 yards. What they didn't want you to know was that those muskets were 74% accurate when fired at a ten foot by ten foot target. No rebel soldier that I knew of was ten feet tall or ten feet wide. I think that would be called "hitting the broad side of a barn."

I was improving my shooting skills everyday with practice. Each time I aimed at the target, I pretended it was the only enemy that I knew personally, Wesley, my brother. I continued to wonder if we would ever get to the war we signed up for. Or if the government just intended to make Company E a bunch of camp loafers.

Sgt. John Culp, an older soldier who was a cousin to my father, was Company E's unofficial chaplain. He led prayer services every Sunday at Camp Scott. He also made sure everyone of boys had their own personal Bible. Some of those books showed regular use. Mine didn't.

John Arendt Sr. left camp this week. He had enlisted in Company E with his two sons, John Jr. and George. It was said the rigors and duties of camps were too severe for his constitution.

In late May, 1861, our officers told us that soon we would be marchin into the South for the first time. We were ordered to break camp. We were to march first to Chambersburg, Pennsylvania. We left on Monday morning and marched all week, arriving in Chambersburg on Friday. When General Patterson arrived by train on Sunday, June 2, a grand parade was held in Chambersburg.

After being there less than a week, I got a telegram that my father had died of paralysis on June 7th. I was shocked by the news. I was able to get a furlough and went back to Gettysburg. Wesley did not return home for the services. That made me just a little more cross with my brother than I already was. Why did he put the war before his family? Why was he splitting the family and fighting – brother against brother? It was Wesley who had left and joined the Confederate Army. I don't know why Wesley was causing our family so much grief.

Father was buried next to my mother. Annie and Julia tried to comfort me, but I was not in the mood. As the oldest in the family, I probably should have tried to comfort them. I would have to mourn some other day. I wasn't ready for such foolishness today.

I got several hours to spend with Salmone before returning to my regiment. She mostly held me. She told me how much she had missed me. My wife admitted that she had perhaps taken me for granted when I was around and didn't realize that until I was gone. She apologized and promised never to do that again. Her tender kisses on that day aroused me beyond belief. But I knew I could not stay.

When I caught up to the Gettysburg boys, our whole Second Division of Patterson's Army was at Williamsport, Maryland, preparing to ford the Potomac River and march into Virginia. I had no accurate count of how many were in with us, but the tents were in long rows in every direction. I could not see the end of the rows as they disappeared over the nearby hills.

The boys from Gettysburg asked about the funeral services. They were sorry they had not been able to attend. They had known my father all their lives too. About all that I could tell them was that Wesley was not there. I was not asked to give a detailed account. I did not tell them how furious I was with my brother for not attending father's memorial.

I wrote home thanking Salmone for her comforting words and touches. Her support had been helpful. I wrote to my sister Annie too. I realized what a burden she had raising Julia by herself.

At Williamsport, Maryland, artillery positions on the bank of the river guarded our men. I heard some one say Captain Abner Doubleday's battery could be trusted with that duty as they were well trained and experienced.

Our boys talked all night about how excited we were to finally face those traitors of the South. Enemy land was right across the river. The enemy would be scrambling to get away from the Union's Second Division in the morning as we would be marching toward them.

General Robert Patterson

Spring, 1861
Johnston Hastings "Jack" Skelly Jr.

Our first days in camp were chaotic. Our commanding officer Brigadier General Wynkoop ordered us to Baltimore aboard the Northern Central Railroad. We only got as far as Ashland Station in Cockeysville, Maryland. There we were informed that the citizens of Maryland, who were pro-secesh, had burned the remaining train bridges all the way to Washington. We camped overnight at Ashland Station surrounded by armed and angry citizens. The next morning, the train returned us to York, Pennsylvania where we set up camp at the York Fairgrounds of the York Agriculture Society known as Camp Winfield Scott. There we were furnished with uniforms that included blue trousers, gray shirt, blue fatigue cap, and a loose blue sack.

We were given a blanket and an overcoat. Our new uniforms were shoddy and not reliable. The pantaloons split after a few days. Our overcoats were flimsey and fell apart to the touch. John McIlhenny of our regiment complained that our uniforms were so shoddy we looked more like convicts than soldiers. He was right. We looked pathetic rather than proud Union soldiers. Our cap was the only part of the uniform that was decent. We talked about how the federal government must have been duped when they hired suppliers to provide uniforms.

When we all appeared at formation the next morning, it was remarkable how we looked much more like soldiers than the day before even in the shoddy new uniforms. We still did not know much about soldiering, but we certainly looked more like we were part of Mr. Lincoln's army.

As for the 2nd Pennsylvania, we were a determined bunch of farmers and merchants. None of us knew anything about soldiering. I was hoping someone in command had a plan to mold us into a fighting unit. I wasn't sure we had it in us.

The officers tried for sure. We started out to be a loose knit bunch, not able to march in a straight line or stop on command. There seemed no hope that we could actually ever be soldiers expected to fight.

I was not sure I wanted to stand next to some of the men in my company even in drills. I could not imagine what they would do if we ever came under actual enemy fire.

We marched back and forth, mostly stepping on each other those first few weeks. It didn't seem like we were improving at all. All we were getting from the exercise was very hungry and very tired. Seemed like the officers thought hungry and tired boys made better soldiers. I was not so certain. We marched two miles an hour. Double stepping got us there faster, but we couldn't keep that up indefinitely because too many boys would drop out from exhaustion.

Our daily schedule was pretty simple. At sunrise we had reveille and roll call followed by breakfast. For breakfast we ate bread and beef. And then we marched and marched, back and forth until mid-day. We rested a few minutes and were given some vittles that included more bread and more beef.

And then we marched a few hours more until supper which consisted of coffee, beans, bread and beef. After supper we had musket practice and then we marched some more. We had roll call at 9 p.m. and then lights out soon after that.

At night we slept in the straw in barns most recently inhabited by cattle. I was usually so tired at the end of the day that I didn't even mind the bad smells that surrounded our beds. We used carpet bags stuffed with straw as pillows.

After a few weeks in camp, I had blisters as big as silver coins all over the bottoms of my feet. There wasn't much to make my sore feet feel better. I knew the next morning I would be marching on those same feet again. My shoes were too big, adding to the blister problem.

Within a few weeks new tents arrived. We were able to move from the cow barns to Sibley tents. The new tents had room enough for thirteen boys and a stove for cooking. William Culp, Edwin, Peter Warren and I all stay in the same tent.

You would have thought after being so tired from the day's marches, we would have just fallen dead to sleep. But several of us stay up late most nights. Those were the times we shared our complaints about the life of a soldier.

The boys complained about the food, the boredom and all the marching. But at the same time, they admitted we didn't act much like soldiers. And that if the rebel army appeared, we would have no idea what to do.

We also practiced the nine-step manual of arms every single day. Our officers said that the procedure to load and fire our muskets must become so familiar that we could do it blindfolded or in our sleep. It would literally be a life saver during battle that this process was totally done without the least bit of thinking on our part. I dreamed at night about loading and firing my musket. They weren't my best dreams.

In mid-May, the fairgrounds was flooded by a terrific rain storm. Almost five inches of water threatened to wash our tents away. Our quarters were moved to South Newberry Street beyond the bridge in York until the water subsided.

I had learned from one of our boys that the whole purpose of the army was to take away the will of every single lad. The officers could not have anyone who wanted to do something individually. That defeated the whole purpose. The idea was to have us all act as one. The officers owned every single move that we made, every single day. Anyone acting alone was acting as a mutineer and was dealt with accordingly. The earlier a soldier figured that out and accepted it, the better off he would be. I accepted it early on. The others were not so accepting.

I wrote regularly to mother, my brother Daniel and to my dear friend Jennie. Writing came easy to me. I wrote more than my brother and that fact got him into trouble with mother.

I wanted to encourage Daniel to be helpful to mother. I knew deep inside he wanted to be a soldier but was too young. That hadn't sat well with him.

As for mother, I wanted her to know I was not in any danger so far. I told her we had not seen the enemy, and didn't expect them to show up soon in York, Pennsylvania. Her letters always asked about my health. I informed her that my health was good and that I was eating well.

Jennie got the most of my attention. I wanted her to know that she was in the front of my thoughts on a regular basis. I told her I missed her, which I did, and that I would continue to watch out for myself so I could return to the comfort of her arms soon. I let her know that I was expecting to be back to Gettysburg no later than July when our ninety day enlistment would be up.

My biggest surprise in all the letters from Gettysburg was the one from my mother saying that my father, who was 48 years old, had enlisted in the 101st Pennsylvania Infantry. I knew how this probably had upset mother. She had not shared how upset she was, but had said there was no discussing his decision. Mother said he just up and left. And I was not sure my brothers Daniel and Edwin were mature enough to have to be the men of the house.

This week the Ladies Relief Society sent shirts and housewives they donated to all our boys camped at York.

The lads here from Gettysburg didn't know much about the actual war. We had not seen it. All we cared about was that we would survive our three month enlistment. After that, we would certainly return home and start where we had left off. It seemed like for now we were not helping President Lincoln win the war.

William talked about his anger with his brother for joining the other side in the war. "Damn, Wesley," he shouted, banging on the table with his fist. "He ain't never done nothing right in his whole life."

I had to say it. "Then why did you expect that he would come home and join the Union army?" I asked, partly as a joke.

But William wasn't joking. He was steaming. He couldn't even look at me. "If I see him, I'm going to shoot him myself," he insisted.

I was taken back by what William said. I might have thought the same way if my brother had joined the rebel army, but I wouldn't have told anyone.

William asked if I would shoot my brother if Edwin were marching with Wesley in the enemy army.

His question took me by surprise. After a few moments of saying nothing, I finally said, "Father and mother taught me better than that. No, I would not shoot my brother."

In fact, I wondered if I could shoot any rebel soldier on purpose. I knew that was what they were training me to do. It was them or me. I was not so inclined to harm anyone. I was not sure when the time came I could be counted on to shoot the enemy.

I was furloughed to return home for three days in mid-May. My approval came so late that I was not able to alert anyone that I was coming. I got to spend time with mother and Jennie. I went home first. Mother cried and hugged me tightly. Daniel and Edwin had all kinds of questions about soldiering.

I gave mother an ambrotype picture. I told my mother, "If I fall in battle, you will know how I looked before this war brought sorrow upon our land." She accepted the picture, while insisting at the same time she would never forgive me if I would "fall in battle." She made me promise I would return home soon. And then, mother cried some more.

Jennie was also quite surprised to see me. We walked down to our favorite spot and lay on a blanket near a stream. We didn't say much. Jennie touched my face and looked at me like she never wanted to forget what I looked like. She cried as she touched me gently.

I gave her an ambrotype picture of me in my uniform I had taken at camp, just like the one I had given to my mother. It showed me sitting in a chair, holding my rifle across my lap. It was a dashing picture if I should say so myself. She held it tight to her bosom, the same bosom she had held me tightly against on several occasions. Then she cried some more.

It was even harder to leave the second time around. Both mother and Jennie cried again and hung on to me as if that was the last hug they might ever get from me.

On May 12, Pennsylvania Governor Curtin reviewed our regiment. We stood over four hours awaiting the review. We were mighty happy when he finally arrived.

Rumors in camp indicated that we might be moving soon to Harpers Ferry, Virginia. But instead, at the end of May, we were ordered to march to Chambersburg, Pennsylvania to prepare for marching into the South.

Our whole company was troubled by the news of the assassination of Colonel Ellsworth in Alexandria, Virginia on May 24. We wanted to avenge the blood he spilled for the cause. We also gave three cheers for General Butler who we were told had captured Nashville. Later we found that rumor was false.

We arrived in Chambersburg on May 28. No provisions arrived to feed us, but the local people were prepared. They took good care of us. In fact, the citizens of Chambersburg were generous with obtaining food for our men.

I took the time to write letters to my brothers Daniel and Edwin, my mother and Jennie. I let them know that we were in Chambersburg and expecting to join the war soon. I promised that I would stay safe, though I was not certain how I could do that in an actual battle. They always seemed to want to know about my health and if I was eating well, so I always assured them that I was healthy at present. Other units arrived over the next few days including the 6th regiment from Schuylkill, Pennsylvania, the 1st Philadelphia including the Scot Legion, the Irish Brigade, and two regiments of Delaware men.

The army gathered at Chambersburg was bigger than any army I had ever seen. Our company E of 100 men was put into the 2nd Brigade, 2nd Division of General Patterson's Union Army.

A new issue of Enfield rifles arrived and we traded our Harpers Ferry muskets for them. The Enfields, from England, were reported to be more accurate than our muskets. We were drilled and trained some more as we camped in Chambersburg. Our officers were quite strict, seriously drilling and training us. We heard the 2nd Regiment had been named the top of all the regiments there as far as military proficiency and intelligence. We would have traded that for seeing a few rebels. We were given extra time to practice and fire our new weapons.

Some of the soldiers took advantage of the people in Chambersburg. Arrests were made for robbery, assault and public drunkenness. We were confined to camp after four of the soldiers brutally killed a colored man who was running a disorderly house the soldiers had been visiting.

On June 2nd following a massive parade down the streets of town, we marched on to Greencastle. We left behind one of the Company E boys, Van Buren Tawney who was ill and left there to recover.

Our army was quite impressive. We had cavalry in the front, followed by infantry and then artillery. We had marched into Greencastle led by four companies of the 2nd U.S. Cavalry.

Those of us in the 2nd Brigade were taken by the Cumberland Valley Railroad to Hagerstown, Maryland. Our march through Hagerstown on June 15 caused great excitement. Major General W. H. Keim led the parade with his troops, followed by our company and with our band playing patriotic tunes. We proceeded to Funkstown.

The day was real hot. The roads were dusty. Men fainted and fell out of line as we marched. Adam Doerson, of Company E, was treated for sunstroke that eventually led to brain fever. He was sent home. We were allowed to purchase crackers, cheese, tobacco, cigars and other items from suttlers.

We each were given coffee, sugar and salt, hardtack and a little pork and beef, which we put in our sacks. The beef was quite inferior. We joked and named it "jerked horse". We each got sixty rounds of ammunition.

At camp some of us were sent out into the town to confiscate federal guns that had found their way into the hands of people leaning toward the South. That afternoon we stood in formation as forty companies were review for both governors -- Pennsylvania Governor Curtin and Maryland Governor Hicks.

The next morning we marched to Williamsport, Maryland. We could see the South across the river. We were anxious to move forward and perhaps end this war. I was hoping our army could to do that within a very short time.

William Culp caught up with us in Williamsport after attending his father's funeral in Gettysburg. He brought news that Van Buren Tawney had never recovered from his illness and had died in Chambersburg.

Camp Scott – York Fairgrounds, York PA
Harpers Weekly, May 25, 1861

Photo Jack Skelly gave to his mother and Jennie

Spring, 1861
Mary Virginia Wade

Life went on in Gettysburg, but it wasn't the same with Jack and the others gone. The women in town followed the war in the newspapers and from the letters they had received from their sons, husbands and boyfriends. To many, those letters were few and far between. Fortunately, Jack was pretty good in keeping me informed. I reread each letter every single night before my night prayers and finally going to bed.

The women here traded the letters between families, or at least informed the others what was in the letters.

I treasured Jack's wisdom. I was sure that he would make someone a wonderful husband. I was just not totally sure at this point why I was waffling on being able to see myself as his wife. I certainly wished to be married someday and to have a wonderful husband. I was not sure what other options I had besides Jack. And deep down, I could not find any fault with Jack at all.

My mother was a big supporter of Jack, though she insisted on calling him Johnston Junior – instead of Jack, like everyone else in town. Could be she just didn't want any mixing up the names, because we called my little brother John James by the name of Jack too. Mother had always encouraged me to stay by Johnston Hastings, because, as she reminded me often, he was everything my father wasn't. Those qualities of Jack certainly would be honor, truthfulness and reliability. My father certainly had none of those.

When I was seven years old, my father was charged with larceny and sent to prison. It was not possible for me to visit, though I begged to see him. He was in the Eastern Penitentiary with no visitors allowed. At that age I did not understand the concept of prison and no visitors allowed and threw several fits. I got nowhere.

If that had been father's only brush with the law, his behavior might have been tolerated. But it wasn't his first and his indiscretions weren't acceptable to my mother. He had been charged with arson, assault and battery at least three different times and with fornication. Mother said he blamed her for his troubles. When he was occasionally freed from jail, she would not allow him to visit. Finally she had him committed to the Adams County Alms House. She said he was "very insane."

I felt sorry for my mother, because she had basically lost my father many years ago when he chose the life of crime over being with his family. "His loss," she would say, not bitterly or angrily, just matter of fact. By this time, I had figured out that if my father had any character, it was at the very least questionable if not down right despicable.

My life now consisted of sewing and cooking for my mother, being there for my sister, helping take care of my younger brothers, and going to church.

I was mighty surprised recently when my best friend, Jack Skelly, showed up unannounced at our front door. He was home on furlough for just a few days. We spent hours and hours getting reacquainted. That included some powerful long hugging and some real nice kissing. I had missed both of those activities. Jack looked pretty good, but didn't seem to like the soldiering much. He promised me he would keep down, stay out of the battles as best he could, and return home to me.

Jack seemed very troubled about William's outward dislike of his brother Wesley. Jack was in the middle, being the best friend of Wesley while being a fellow soldier of William. Jack shared with me that if it came down to one of the brothers or the other, he would have no problem siding with Wesley on any question whatsoever. Jack called Wesley a man of character, someone who could be trusted, and a true friend. He would not have said anything of the sort about William.

My friend, Jack, gave me a handsome photograph showing him in his uniform. After he left to go back to camp, I began clutching that photograph often. I missed Jack already. But I also knew deep down inside, that in order for our love to grow, we must experience this time apart.

I was not sleeping well at all. I worried about all the Gettysburg boys and about my long lost father. I worried about my future, my sister, Georgia, and the other women of Gettysburg whose husbands and sons had gone off to war.

Jack wrote me a letter from Chambersburg letting me know that he was in good health. He said each day they were getting closer to going into the war that they had not been a part of up to this time. I feared for his safety even when he assured me that he would stay back and be safe.

In early June, William and Wesley's father passed away. My sister, mother and I attended the services. Annie and Julia were quite shaken as they had lost both their mother and father recently. They were also quite upset that their brother Wesley was not there. Annie told me he could not get a pass to come into the North.

I talked to William who came home from the funeral. William assured me that they had been in no danger, but the Gettysburg boys were now somewhere around Chambersburg, Pennsylvania and in camp, preparing to march into the South. He said they were excited to finally get a chance to put into use all the drilling they had practiced in camp at York.

Part III

Summer 1861
John Wesley Culp

On July 1st, we were told that we would be movin out from Camp Stephens the next mornin. It was said the enemy was comin our way. The mood in camp changed instantly from boredom to excitement. Finally we would get to face the Yanks in battle.

John and I vowed to stay together through the day, to watch each other and to guard our backs. We were awakened in the night and ordered to march towards Falling Waters, further north of our camp.

The night was much brighter than usual, as a comet was visible all across the sky. I had never seen one before. Our boys took it as a good sign that God was smiling down on our rebel boys.

We were told the Union army was crossin the Potomac River at Williamsport, Maryland and was enterin Virginia. We were bein sent to help delay their march into Virginia, to give them an unfriendly welcome and to halt their invasion into the South.

We marched with more bounce in our steps that day than any day before this. We were finally goin to see some action.

When we started marchin, we were also eatin lots of dirt and dust on a hot, hot day in Virginia. Along the way we were stopped and deployed on a ridge.

Captain Pendleton's battery placed three guns along the road. He marched forward with one six pounder and six men.

The boys of Company B, 2nd Virginia Volunteer Infantry were ordered by Colonel James Allen to count off in twos. John was a one. I was a two. The ones formed up an arc on a small knoll on the left side of the road. Those of us who were twos lined up behind them. The idear was to have the second row fill in between the spaces in the first row. It was a formation we had practiced drillin many times before. The 4th Virginia boys were set up in the same formation on the right side of the road.

Our orders were to load our muskets and stand ready. But we were not to shoot until the order was given. We were told the federal boys did not know we were awaitin for them. Our first shots would be a big surprise.

Colonel Jackson took the 5th Virginia and marched them forward, where they formed up a good ways in front of us. The artillery battery joined them at the front. The 1st Virginia Cavalry supported the 5th Virginia on their left. We were able to see their lines from our position on the field.

We didn't have to wait too long. Captain Pendleton's cannon fired a shell welcomin the federal boys into Virginia. Another cannon shell was fired in the direction of the federals. Soon the federal guns answered, sending artillery shells over our front lines, but fallin harmlessly in front of us. Actually the shells were closer to Colonel Jackson who was observing on a ridge about halfway between our lines, our Cavalry, and 5th Virginia boys, but the shells fell behind them and in front of us.

As the federals got closer, our boys out front fell back. We were ordered to do the same. Later we were told our men were greatly outnumbered by the Union boys and that Colonel Jackson was just buyin time for the boys back at Camp Stephens to abandon camp.

We fell back, watchin our rear at all times. We were stayin alert due to the federal boys bein in pursuit.

I was disappointed that we were given the order to retreat without ever receivin the order to fire our muskets. We were never called into battle.

And even though Company B saw no action and suffered no casualties, for the first time we got to see the war. Our brigade did suffered its first casualty as George Roup of the 5th Virginia was killed in action and left on the field.

"Maybe next time they will ask us to step into the fray," I thought as we marched south again.

We marched past Camp Stephens and formed our lines across another ridge to await the federal troops and harass them some more. After an hour or so, they didn't show up. We marched through Martinsburg, spending the night at Big Spring just south of town.

The followin morning we set up camp at Darkesville.

Henry Kyd Douglas stopped at camp. He had been at the front of the battle and said "there for the first time I heard the whiz of a musket ball and the shriek of cannon shot." He said it was a frightenin experience. I had not been close enough to either to have been frightened.

We celebrated the Fourth of July with the news that federal soldiers in Martinsburg entered a house to demand that the residents give up their rebel flags. The lady of the house refused. When the Yankee soldiers threatened to arrest her, the lady's daughter shot the Yankee and killed him. The young girl had been arrested. Our men wanted to march back into Martinsburg and get her out of jail.

We also cheered the news that Colonel Jackson was now General Jackson.

The next mornin we heard that the young girl had been released. We cheered the courage of the young girl we found out was Belle Boyd. Ben Boyd from our regiment's Company D knew her quite well. He was Belle's father.

I quietly celebrated my 22nd birthday. No one here knew it was my birthday ceptin me. I wasn't going to tell them. I was excited to be 22 and happy to be alive. No one ever knew what the next day would have in store.

For four days we formed up and waited for the Yanks to come toward Darkesville. They never arrived. On the fourth day Brigadier General Johnston's forces arrived from Winchester to fortify our ranks. Johnston took some of our companies and marched toward Winchester. We followed, campin in Bunker Hill.

The 2nd Virginia Volunteer Infantry received orders on July 11 to march to Winchester. We were to prepare to face General Patterson's Union troops, those same Yankees we had seen from afar in the small fight on July 2. This time we was itchin to fight and see if all the drillin had paid off. Our boys waited and waited. And we waited some more. General Patterson's Union men did not show up. The mood of our men this time was disappointment. Our day would come. It just was not to be today.

On July 18, our camp was buzzin with the news that another part of the federal army was at Manassas Junction, Virginia. We were needed to help defend Virginia against their invasion. We cheered the news as we prepared to break camp.

Our regiment marched east, crossin the Blue Ridge Mountains at Ashby's Gap. Although the day was very hot, the men had a new purpose. Our march was upbeat. We were finally goin to the war that we had all signed up to be a part of. And, of course, we had no idea what we were in for. We camped at the pass, with General Jackson keepin us mindful of a possible attack from the rear.

We waded the Shenandoah River at Berry's Ferry. To most men the water was chilly and chest high. To me, one of the smallest soldiers in the 2nd Virginia, the water was up to my chin and nose. Men to my right and left helped me across. They laughed, sayin that they would hate to lose me to the waters of the river before I got a chance to shoot my first Union soldier. I was not laughin. I was just tryin to survive the river crossin.

The cold water felt good on a very hot day. It served as the only bath us boys had in several weeks.

We had not even dried off when we were herded onto freight and cattle cars at Piedmont just as the sun came up on the mornin of July 19. We rode on the train all day.

The cars bumped along as we lay in the dark, too crowded to move. There was no fresh air. Most of the men around me were asleep. The situation was almost unbearable. But it sure was a nice change from havin to march twenty or thirty miles a day.

We got off the train at Mitchell's Ford in the late evenin. We marched down the road toward Manassas Junction. With each step we were marchin closer to the fightin we had signed up for. Our officers expected a battle within the next few days. One hundred rounds of ammunition were given to each of us.

Was this better than the borin routine we were tired of? Why were we lookin forward to a battle when we had no idea of the outcome?

I wondered that night as I stayed awake with the others, cleanin my musket. No one knew what we were in for in the days ahead. I thought of my sisters back home in Gettysburg. I thought of John's wife, Mary, in Shepherdstown. I even wondered where my brother, William, and my friend, Jack Skelly, were in their part of the war.

No one in camp slept. Some prayed out loud. I heard boys cryin. There was fear in the camp, but I was not afraid. I just wondered what was goin to happen. I had never liked the unknown. I certainly was facin it tonight.

Men talked about just about everythin that evenin, but strangely no one talked about what tomorrow might be like. We knew what we were trained to do. I thought we would perform well as we were certainly more like real soldiers than we had been just a few months before. I had only seen a small battle at Falling Waters. And I saw that from a distance. No bullets or cannons had been fired at Company B.

Drillin was only one part of our trainin. None of us had ever had someone shootin at us and tryin to kill us while we were goin through the nine steps to load and shoot our muskets. Certainly the battles would be much more interestin than just marchin and drillin. And certainly more interestin than any day in Shepherdstown. And a lot more dangerous too.

I asked God to watch out for me and the men of Company B on the morrow. I have not always been a man of a lot of prayer on a regular basis. I figured if Company B ever needed to be watched over by God, tomorrow might be that day.

I didn't know how brave I would be in battle. I wondered about the boys to my right and left. I was not sure who I could count on if we came under enemy fire. I had no doubt about my officers. I admired Brigadier General Johnston and General Jackson. I would follow them anywhere.

General Johnston led us onto the field at Manassas Junction on the morning of July 21. We could hear that the fightin had already begun. We marched maybe four miles to the top of a small hill near a farmhouse. Colonel Allen ordered us to form a line on the left of the brigade to assist the rebel left. It was around noon when we got to our position. The 33rd Virginia anchored the line on our left.

It wasn't but a few minutes after we formed up that rebel soldiers already battered and wounded limped past our line, movin toward the rear. And then the federal guns started poundin our line from a nearby hill. The noise was deafenin. We ducked down and held our position.

We awaited orders. None came. I think we were under attack for maybe ninety minutes. None of the cannon shots hit our lines, though the ground was shakin all around us. It seemed like we were in a real bad situation. They were firin at us and we were not fightin back. But I trusted that my officers knew that we really were not in much danger if we stayed where we were.

When the federal cannons finally fell silent, I was relieved. But the quiet was short lived. Next time their guns started firin, the artillery pieces had been moved to the same ridge our line was on. And it seemed we were in big trouble.

Just then I heard the command we had been waitin for. Colonel Allen's voice boomed as loud as the cannons. "Charge and take the battery."

At the same time the 33rd Virginians fixed their bayonets and advanced on the battery. We yelled and screamed as we poured onto the ridge. Their attack opened our lines to enemy fire. Company's C and G took the brunt of the attack. I saw Captain William Nelson (Company C) shot in his chest. Blood squirted out of his uniform front. I was sick, but stayed alert. We were takin direct fire too.

Our boys went through the drill. We loaded and fired, just as we had been taught. It came easy cause we had done it so many times. I was doin the drill, and not really payin attention to what happened after my shot. I was loadin for another. The reality set in when I saw a young federal lad take a shot to the face right in front of us.

I don't know what I was expectin, watchin that lad's face suddenly turn red as blood flowed. He fell on his face and did not move. A bad taste rose in my throat. I fought back tryin not to get sick. I needed to concentrate on the drill of loadin my musket and firin. There was no time to think of that poor Yankee boy, someone's son or brother, who our lads had just killed.

Yet I thought about him more as I tried to put him out of my mind. Funny how our minds do that when we least expect it. Somehow I got my focus back and continued to fire on the enemy line.

A bit later, Colonel Allen ordered us to fall back and reform. We scampered back and formed up at his command. We charged the federal flank. In the smoke and fire, the companies around us seemed to be confused. Some fell back to join our lines. We listened for another command, but none came. John, who was on my right, pointed to Colonel Allen. The Colonel seemed to not know where he was. (Later we learned that he had been poked in the eye by a tree branch and was temporarily blind.) One of our men went to his aid. He got Colonel Allen to a safe position behind our line.

Lt. Francis Lackland rallied our brigade, addin his one hundred men to the nearby 4th Virginia. Together we charged the battery but were stopped by the federals and pushed back.

The 2nd Virginia Volunteer Infantry, in spite of the large amount of casualties, held our ground proudly. We had seen our first fight. Our regiment had seen its first casualties. But we had proudly not backed down to anythin the federals had thrown at us.

I was told later that the federals almost ruled the day, but in the end, they were runnin back to Washington – soundly defeated. The boys from the South had won.

Company B had survived the battle with no casualties -- none dead, none wounded and none missin. The 2nd Virginia had not fared as well, sufferin fifteen dead and fifty three wounded.

One of those wounded boys was a Shepherdstown lad, Fitzhugh Lee, who was shot in the chest. He had mustered into the 33rd Virginia regiment. With his death several days later, he left a widow Lily, who was daughter of Doctor Richard and Laura Parran of Shepherdstown.

The boys of Company B and the 2nd Virginia Volunteer Infantry can look back to July 21, 1861 at the battle at Manassas Junction as the day Colonel Allen predicted would come – the day we had finally become soldiers.

I look back on it as the day I saw my first dead Yankee soldier. What I thought would be a proud moment and a thrill, was not either one. I wanted to write the boy's mother and tell her how sorry I was that we had killed her son. I wanted to tell her how sorry I was about this whole damn war. Of course, I did not know his name. I needed to put him behind me. But it wasn't as easy as that.

We all grieved Fitzhugh Lee's death because he was one of us. Although we all knew any of us could die any day, the reality of havin to bury one of our boys from Virginia did not set well with us. We had lost George Roup at Fallin Waters but he had died on the field. We had no chance to retrieve his body for burial. We were hit harder by Lee's death.

What I didn't tell anyone in camp was that I had shot my first Yankee soldier. I don't know if I killed him or not. He was takin aim at my captain who had his back turned. The federal soldier didn't see me. He was only about twenty yards from where I was standin. He shot at the captain and missed just as I shot. But I didn't miss. He fell and didn't move.

We marched on soon after that. It wasn't my place to check on the lad or ask his forgiveness. This was war. It was kill or be killed. I didn't even tell my captain that I had perhaps saved his life. It didn't matter. What mattered was that I was alive and my captain was alive. My trainin had paid off too. But that didn't keep me from relivin the moment over and over again. I was not feelin good at all about my first killin of another boy, about my age. I wondered if someday someone would have the same feelins after havin just shot me dead.

As for me, I was not tellin anyone that I had bad feelins about it. I know I did right by shootin him.

General Jackson, I am sure, would have been proud of me. But I would have been court martialled and probably shot if anyone knew how badly I felt about killin a Yankee.

We set up our tents at Camp Harman near Centreville after the battle. I was mighty happy we had won our first major fight. The boys of Company B talked that evenin that this battle would end the war.

Word came back to us that because of our stand at Bull Run, General Thomas J. Jackson was given the name "Stonewall" by a newspaper reporter who had heard General Bee say that "Jackson was standing like a stone wall." The general was said to be embarrassed by the name and said the name "Stonewall" should be given to his men. Our brigade became known as the Stonewall Brigade. It was a name we carried proudly.

In late August, we learned that Lt. Colonel Lackland had checked himself into a hospital at Fairfax Court House complainin of chest pains and a severe cough. On September 4th we were saddened to hear that he had died.

Life at Camp Harman brought back memories of the days before we had become real soldiers. The drills and marchin returned. Day after day – mornin, noon and night -- we marched and drilled. Durin the whole time, the war went on somewhere else. The 2nd Virginia was not part of it.

But this time, we had seen war and had been a part of it. And I did not like what I saw. This time I did not complain that we were bein left behind.

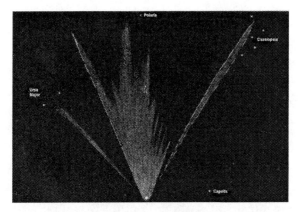

Great Comet of 1861

Summer 1861
William Esaias Culp

We were sent to our tents early on the night of July 1. Tomorrow early we would be finally crossin into the South. We were called to formation about two o'clock in the morning. As we prepared to march, General Patterson spoke, standing on a stump and shouting so he could be heard.

> Men. I am very proud of you. In a tight place, I expect every man here to help me out. Today we will begin a massive attack on the secessionist states of the South. I would rather like to settle these difficulties peacefully if possible and if not, any way we can do it.
>
> The states we are moving into are responsible for trying to break our Union apart. We cannot let that happen. President Lincoln knows that we are about to cross this river behind me. His thoughts and prayers are with us. When we cross the river, we will be in the South. You will not be welcomed there. In fact, everyone, from the oldest man and woman to the youngest child, is your enemy. Do not take any life except that of a rebel soldier, but be aware that even a woman or a child can wield a weapon and shoot you just as dead.
>
> Look around you and seriously consider that the men to your right or left, your long time friends from home, may not survive this day. And you might not survive this day either.
>
> We are here for the greater good – to preserve the Union. There is no room for failure. We have a job to do. And we will do it.

Fight as if your life depended on it, because it does. You are a well-trained, fighting force. You have been drilled and are well prepared. You are ready for whatever happens today and tomorrow. In the heat of the battle, rely on your instincts and your training. It will get you through the day. You are not trained to think or make decisions. You are trained to obey your orders. Do that and we will be victorious.

And now men, as we march into Virginia, may we pause just a moment and ask the great God to bless the men in the federal army."

After a few silent moments of prayer, the order was given and the 2nd Division began crossing the river into the South.

The bright light of a comet lighted the sky. We took it as a positive sign that God blessed our river crossing and was on our side.

Company E waited our turn. I watch curiously as McMullin's Independent Rangers led the federal army across, fording the river and climbing the bank on the other side. They were an interesting bunch we had encountered several days back. These boys were all volunteer firemen from Philadelphia – the Moyamensing Hose Company.

Their uniforms were distinctive, to say the least. They wore gray uniforms with black trim and a white cloth hanging from their hats so as to protect the back of their necks from sunburn. Their unit drew a few shots from the other bank. I wondered if their unique uniforms had drawn the attention from the rebels.

Our company finally received orders to ford the Potomac River at about four o'clock in the morning on July 2, 1861. We sat on the Maryland shore and stripped from the waist down. We were told the water would be chest high and that we needed to hold our clothing and equipment high over our heads as we crossed.

In the daylight, the sight of our men, naked from the waist down would have been a sight to see. The darkness covered up some of the embarrassment although the comet brightened the night sky.

The water was very cold. For a minute or two the water felt very good on my achin feet. The current was swift. Several men were carried down stream and had to be retrieved by others.

On the southern shore we scrambled to get dressed and catch up with the men in front of us. As I looked back, the scene of half naked men crossing the river holding everything they owned above them was quite comical.

We formed up in twos marching down the road. Some of the cavalry peeled off and took through the woods to our right. The heat was quite oppressive. We stopped to fill our canteens at a pretty little water falls called Falling Waters.

As new recruits who had practiced to be soldiers, we really did not know what to expect. But all of us knew we were no longer in the North. In crossing the river, we had crossed the dividing line. We were now in enemy territory.

None of us had ever been to battle. Secretly, I hoped that I would be brave. I was not sure being brave was possible with cannon shot and minie balls whizzing by me. We were trained to fight. But I was not sure the real thing would be the same as what we were taught in camp.

The lads from Gettysburg closed ranks. We marched silently down a narrow road. We had not been told of our destination. We just shouldered our arms and followed directly behind the lads in front of us. I wondered when the action would begin.

Some days we ate as much dust from the roads as anything else. Today we ate dust with every step we took. We marched steadily until almost nine in the morning. We were hoping for a rest due to us soon. Instead there was artillery fire in front of us. Musket fire followed. I was startled at first. Then I was excited. This is what we had been training for. *Bring them on*, I thought.

We were ordered into the woods to our right, to form lines and stand ready. Four artillery pieces were called to the front, passing along side our company.

The 1st Wisconsin and the 11th Pennsylvania were deployed out front as skirmishers.

Where we were standing in our lines, we could hear the cannons and see the smoke. But we did not know if the artillery fire was from the federals or the rebels.

I personally wanted to run to the front to help our boys fight. But I knew that my place was to wait for orders. For Company F, the orders never came.

Whatever happened in front of us, our boys pushed forward. The rebels ran from the fight. We had won the day. We suffered only a few casualties including one killed and six wounded, all but one from the 1st Wisconsin. A Pennsylvania lad, Amos Zuppinger, had been killed in action, the first Pennsylvania soldier to die in battle.

Our cavalry that had looped around to come in from the flank, had been surprised by the rebel cavalry. Forty-five of our cavalry men were captured.

I thought that what happened hadn't been that bad. But I certainly would have felt differently if one of those cannon balls or minie balls had hit me.

Following the fighting, we marched to a camp nearby that the rebels had abandoned recently. We were happy to find a stash of new tents they had left in haste of avoiding the federal army. Many of our boys took their tents cause we didn't have our own.

We stayed for two nights and then marched into Martinsburg, Virginia on the morning of July 4. Some of our soldiers took down Confederate flags on the poles there and replaced them with the U.S. flag -- the red, white, and blue -- indicating our occupation. A federal soldier was shot and killed by a civilian woman in town during our short stay. I remembered that General Patterson had told us that we were now in hostile territory. We were told to be aware that everyone, even women and children, were our enemy.

Jack Skelly told me during our time in Martinsburg that Wesley's unit had been with the rebel regiment we had faced when we crossed the river. They had just fled from Martinsburg before we arrived. *Too bad*, I thought to myself. *I would like to have taken a shot at him with my trusty rifle on the very first day we entered the South.*

We stayed in camp for a week. We were told that General Patterson was awaiting further orders. Rumors flew that we were marching into action in Winchester, Virginia soon. Our company was excited about the possibility of finally seeing some action.

When our supply wagons caught up with us, we were finally fed. We got three meals a day. We had lived since Williamsport on hardtack and coffee. Finally when we did march again, instead of marching to face the enemy in Winchester, we marched to Charlestown. We camped there on July 17.

The postmaster finally caught up with us in Charlestown. I quickly opened and read a very welcomed letter from my wife Salmon. She talked of my recent visit. She told me how she missed me terribly.

I wrote back telling her of our entry into the South at Williamsport, Maryland and how we over ran a unit of Virginians that included my brother. I assured her I was not near the action.

I also sent a letter to Annie. I had promised to send her money but our paymaster had not arrived since the day we enlisted. It was important to assure her that I was not in any danger.

There was no enemy in Charlestown except for heavy rains. We camped there for several days. Word got back to us that General Patterson had blundered by not ordering us to Winchester. General Patterson's mistake had allowed the rebels to escape. Because of that, General Patterson was relieved of his command. In his farewell remarks, he spoke favorably of our regiment, saying that we had "steadily advanced in the face of the enemy." I was not sure if he was talking about us or confusing us with some unit he had led in another war.

One of our Company E boys, Henry D. Ziegler, contracted asthma in Charlestown as a result of all the rain.

On July 26 we were shipped by cars to Harrisburg, Pennsylvania and were mustered out. For Company E the war was over. When we arrived home in Gettysburg, we basked in the attention of the home folks who treated us like heroes. Everyone wanted to know what the war was like.

My time with Salmone was wonderful. I visited Julia and Annie, allowing them to check me out to make sure I was all in one piece.

But since I had not seen much of the action, I was troubled answering their questions. I was also uncomfortable receiving their tributes. I didn't feel much like our company had helped President Lincoln even a lick. I actually gave thought to re-enlisting.

I talked with the others. Many had the same thoughts as I did. I finally made the decision to join up again. To everyone else, the decision was theirs. Before I had a chance to talk to them, Jack Skelly took charge. He stood up and gave a fine speech, letting every one of the Gettysburg boys know just what the situation was and why we should all sign up again. I was proud of Jack doing that.

Not everyone bought Jack's arguments. Some of the Worth Infantry, the York Rifles, and even some of the Independent Blues decided they liked the quiet at home and stayed.

I was bored. I had not joined to march and drill. I had enlisted to fight the enemy and save the Union. The minor battle after crossing the Potomac River had not counted as a real battle. We had not fought anyone yet.

I would not have bet that all our boys would be in for the long haul. After Jack's talk, several from Company E signed up again.

On September 25, 1861, the Gettysburg boys enlisted or reenlisted for a three year term, this time as Company F of the 87th Pennsylvania Infantry. Along with myself and Jack

Skelly were John and Elias Sheads, William Baker, William McGonigal, Peter Warren, Franklin D. Daphoen, Duncan Little, George "Temp" Little, Theodore Norris, and John Arnedt Jr. reenlisted. And other local men David Myers, Edwin Skelly (Jack's brother) H.H.H. Welch, William T. Ziegler, Jacob Rice, William Holtzman, and William Weikert joined us. With my re-enlistment, I was appointed the company's orderly sergeant.

Company F was one of ten local companies, eight from York County and two from Adams County. We were now under the command of Major Charles H. Buehler.

On September 28, we changed station from Camp Scott in York, Pennsylvania and traveled by North Central Railroad to Cockeysville, Maryland. It was over forty miles. I was thankful that we didn't have to march that distance.

I received another letter from Salmone. She had looked in on Annie and Julia and was keeping an eye on them while I was gone. I was grateful for that. I wrote to her from York telling her of my new appointment and that I was eligible for a pay raise. Of course that was up to the pay master who we had not seen even once since our April enlistment. I told her I was pleased that her brother John had stopped by to see me.

My sister Annie had also sent a letter that I received in York, Pennsylvania. I answered her with some of the same information I had passed on to Salmone. I apologized again that I could not send money and wondered how Annie was able to take care of Julia without my financial help.

Battle of Falling Waters – *Harpers Weekly* July 27, 1861

Summer 1861
Jonathan Hastings "Jack" Skelly Jr.

General Patterson set the tone for the river crossing. He told us of the importance of our mission. He spoke of the training we had received and how that would carry each of us through the day.

Company E moved into the South in the very early morning hours of July 2. The crossing was lit by a comet that appeared brightly in the night sky. Our boys waded the ford while others downstream crossed on a pontoon bridge at Williamsport, Maryland. Even in the dark the crossing was less dignified as you might have thought. All our boys stripped naked from the waist down to keep our equipment dry. We held everything high over our heads as we crossed.

On the other side we had to re-dress before falling in line. If the rebels had attacked at any time during the river crossing a lot of our boys would have gone to their final resting place buck naked except for their shirts.

I was told about 14,200 soldiers marched with us that day in the 2nd Division of the Union army under the command of General Robert Patterson. We were an impressive looking fighting force of federal soldiers. President Lincoln, I was sure, would have been proud to see our army this day.

As we marched, some of our boys slipped into the woods and brought luscious blackberries for the rest of us. At a short stop at a fine little water falls, I sipped the cold water and filled my canteen. The day was very hot.

I wasn't expecting that the fight would come to us that day, but we had marched only about five hours into the South, when the sounds of a battle reached Company E, about half way back in the federal column. We were set to formation, awaiting our officers to give us the command.

The thunder of cannons, the smell of smoke, the sounds of minie balls, and the screams of fighting men were all that we experienced. Our men were ordered to double quick step for several miles before being halted. We could not see anything in front of us. We stayed back and waited. Other companies were commanded forward. Company E was not.

The battle was won. The rebels fled the scene. We were happy about that. We were not needed today. But we had to be ready for whatever was coming next.

I was told that our casualties for the day were "very light". General Patterson's army losses were minimal but we had forty five captured from our cavalry. One boy from Pennsylvania was among those who died, killed by a minie ball. I suppose if I had been one on that list, I certainly would not have considered the action to be "very light" at all.

Our first action was exciting but scary. I can't say any shots were fired directly at me, but just the idea of having someone standing across the field firing at men on the other side was not the least bit appealing for me.

I trusted my boys from Gettysburg but was not so sure about the other lads. I would have taken a bullet for my boys, and given my life for the cause. But the cause had gotten lost over the last few months. It seemed that everything was becoming blurred. At least that was the case for me.

After the battle we camped two nights at the old rebel camp. I picked up a new rebel tent left in their haste of facing our federal army. It was my first booty of the war.

On the morning of July 4, we captured the town of Martinsburg in the northern part of Virginia. There was no opposition to our arrival. Pickets were set up at the edges of town. The boys of our company were dismissed for the rest of the day. I set out to see if I could find out something about my friend, Wesley Culp, who I had heard was now working in Martinsburg.

I walked around, asking several men if they knew of a carriage business in Martinsburg. The first two times I asked, the men acted like they were deaf. They looked at me but did not respond. I guess they were not happy that a Union soldier was talking to them. I did not blame them. In fact, I found it rather amusing since they had started the war and we were merely trying to end it.

On my third try, I got pointed in the right direction. I walked to the John C. Allen Coach Shop. The men working on carriages stopped to see what I wanted. They did not seem happy that the federal army was in Martinsburg. I assured them I was not going to trouble them. I just had a few questions.

"Do you know Wesley Culp?" I asked.

"Of course," one admitted. "He worked in this shop until the war came. Is he in trouble?"

"No. He is my best friend," I told them. "I grew up with him in Gettysburg. Do you know where I could find him?"

"He's with the Hamtramck Guards. They are now part of the 2nd Virginia brigade. They just marched through here heading south, just before your men came into town," the man said.

We must have faced his boys in the recent skirmish, I thought. At least he got away. I did not apologize. In fact, I felt pleased he had avoided our fire. But as big as this war was, I found it almost impossible to imagine in our first opportunity to fight the rebels, we had somehow already faced Wesley's company.

I found William and told him what I had discovered. I wasn't sure William was pleased or not that we had just missed his little brother.

Letters were waiting for me at camp from mother and Jennie. I wrote to mother first assuring her that I was safe after my first encounter with the war. I informed her that we were well back of the fighting and didn't actually see much except smoke. I probably surprised her by telling her that Wesley Culp was in the enemy army that opposed us in the battle. For such a huge war, it seems quite a coincidence that my friend was on the other lines.

I told Jennie much the same. I wanted her to know that although we were close to the battle at hand, I was not in any danger whatsoever. She did not need to have to worry about me as I could take care of myself. Besides, I would be coming home shortly. I told her that too.

We set up camp. I was enjoying my new rebel tent. It looked to me like it was brand new.

General Patterson held council of war with his staff on July 9 in Martinsburg. All eleven staff officers voted to withdraw to Charlestown rather than pursuing the rebel boys into Winchester that General Patterson had recommended.

After camping in Martinsburg longer than a week, we marched out, leaving three regiments to guard Martinsburg. We marched a few miles south to set up camp at nearby Charlestown on the July 17.

General Patterson was relieved of command at Charlestown. Word is that we were supposed to block the rebels escape to Winchester instead of marching to Charlestown.

I received a letter from Jennie telling me that they had heard at home that one of the soldiers from Pennsylvania had died at the battle on July 2. I had not known that myself. I smiled when she said postal officials in Gettysburg thought she was getting more mail from the war than anyone in town. My return letter to her let her know again that I was safe.

By the end of July, our ninety day enlistment period had expired. We were shipped by cars to Harrisburg and walked home to Gettysburg.

Mother, Daniel, Edwin and Jennie were all quite happy to see me. They wanted to know everything about the war. I didn't have many answers as we hadn't seen much of the war at all. In fact, I was embarrassed that the town made such a fuss over us Gettysburg boys.

In Gettysburg we were treated like returning warriors, even though our war experience was much more a tale of marching and drilling. The skirmish near Falling Waters where we were far away from any danger could not possibly have been counted as battle experience.

By mid-August many of us were itching to leave again to re-enlist. Edwin especially wanted to go this time. Even William Culp was leaning toward going back into the army.

We decided to hold a meeting amongst the Independent Blues in Gettysburg to discuss re-enlistment as a group. I asked to speak to the boys before we decided what to do. Here's what I told them.

I am certainly no speaker or preacher. In fact, I have never done this before. But I have been thinking about what enlisting has meant to me since we were mustered in. Here's what I wanted to tell you.

This war is not about you and it is not about me. This war is about our country; the United States of America. Our country is being threatened by a bunch of states who want to go have their own country. All of us signed up in April to save our country because Mr. Lincoln, the man who the country elected to be our president, called for us to help.

Every boy here represents a good Gettysburg family. In my family, when I joined, my father joined Company K of the 101st Pennsylvania Infantry. And my brothers Daniel and Edwin are chomping at the bit to join. So I figure the Skelly family's doing our share.

The Sheads family has two boys here, John and Isaac. Both of the Culp boys marched off to war. Many other families sent boys to be repre-sented in Company E of the 2nd Pennsylvania Volunteers. I am proud to stand on any field of battle with any one of you.

Our enlistment has ended. We have a choice. We can re-enlist or stay here at home. No one here will say anything about it if you want to stay in Gettysburg– and I will make sure of that. But I am re-enlisting and fighting until the end. This coun-try is still in danger. This war is not over. I am not a quitter. I will not quit on my responsibility to my country.

Now you can certainly say that your responsibility has ended – that you stayed as long as you signed up for. And with that you are right. If we all stay home, we can say we did our part. Our family and neighbors will probably treat us like heroes. But we ain't heroes yet, cause the work is not finished. Some days I don't feel like we are helping our country at all, just marching here and there. But if we don't re-enlist, I figure we will be hurting our country. I don't want to be any part of that.

I remember reading in school about our founding fathers back in 1776. They wanted their freedom. They thought that freedom was worth fighting for. They gave their lives so that we could be part of the United States. One even said, and you will have to forgive me cause I cannot remember who that person was, "Give me liberty or give me death." We too are fighting for our freedom. And we are fighting this fight to the death. Some of us will not survive. Others of us will return home missing arms or legs. Some of us will die of disease. But it cannot be said of anyone who signs up for more that he did not give his all to protect our freedoms and to save our country.

You can like me or hate me for saying this. You can cheer me or swear at me. I do not care. Terrible things have been happening to boys our own age on both sides. In the recent battle we just watched, we had several casualties. Already several lads from the 2nd Division have given the ultimate sacrifice for their country.

But we have not given enough, cause the war has not been won. I think we will win. I cannot tell you how soon that will happen. My brother Edwin and I are signing up for the newly authorized 87th Pennsylvania regiment. William Culp is re-enlisting. Our next stop is to sign the papers.

If you are with us, I will watch your back in battle, as I expect you will watch mine. I will share my tent and my rations with you. I will fight fiercely to win this war and to win it soon so that we can all come back home. I will not promise anything more than that. If you stay home today, I wish you well. And I hope to God that when this war is over, you will have a country to live in where you are still free.

With that I walked to the recruiting tent of the 87th Pennsylvania and signed my name. I did not stick around to see who was with me and who was going home. I had said my piece. I had done what I could.

I was real proud that many of the Gettysburg boys came by to let me know they appreciated what I said. Two said they were not sure what decision to make. My talk helped them decide to stay. Several joined Company C of the Maryland Potomac Home Brigade.

Nicholas Codori, who was married and had small children, told me he was tired of everything and was staying home. I had no hard feelings. We shook hands and wished each other well. And Louis McClellan, who was engaged to Jennie's sister, decided to stay home too.

William and Edwin teased me, telling me I should be a preacher or an officer. They said that my talk had been real good. And they thought all the Gettysburg boys who stayed had re-enlisted due to my words of inspiration.

With my signature came a promotion. I was now Corporal Johnston Hastings "Jack" Skelly, Jr.

We were sent to York to the already familiar fairgrounds at Camp Scott to begin training as a new regiment. Shortly after that we were moved by rail to Cockeysville, and then to Lutherville, Maryland where we set up our winter camp.

In my letters to mother and Jennie I explained that I had enlisted again and was now Corporal Johnston H. Skelly, Jr. Company F of the 87th Pennsylvania Infantry. That allowed me a little more money in my pay, but we had not been paid since the day we enlisted. I warned them that several of the Gettysburg soldiers were staying home and told them they were heroes. No one was to bother them for not re-enlisting.

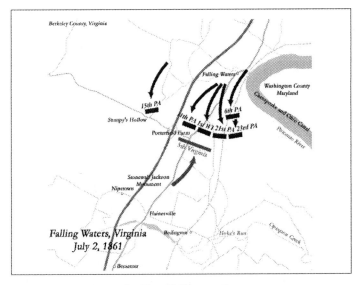

www.battleoffallingwaters.com

Wesley's unit was behind the 5th Virginia near
Nipetown and Hainesville

William and Jack's unit was in the rear of
the Union lines near Falling Waters

Summer 1861
Mary Virginia Wade

The heat of the summer bore down upon Gettysburg. I was sure it was bearing down on our Gettysburg boys somewhere too. Those wool uniforms could not be real comfortable in the summer heat.

We had gotten only a little information on where the Gettysburg boys were since they have left home. Jack's letters have been helpful in letting me know at least that I am missed. Recently I received letters telling of their marching into the South.

I was not familiar with places like Martinsburg and Charlestown, Virginia where they had been. Jack's early letters talked of the boredom of training. But he knew they were inexperienced and needed the instruction. Jack was not comfortable with his being a soldier. He said others were.

His latest letter told of the regiment's marching into the South near Martinsburg. That was where Wesley Culp was now working. It was Wesley's regiment that had been pushed back by the Pennsylvania boys.

I wrote back and told him how proud I was of what he was doing for his country.

Everyone had predicted the war would not last long. But already it had been going on for more than three months. I had read in the newspapers that at the battle at Manassas Junction, people dressed up all fancy and took picnics to watch the fighting. But then when the battle began, they were so terrified that they abandoned their fancy parties and high-tailed it back to Washington City. I cannot imagine wanting to watch boys fight and die before your eyes. That was not appealing to me in the least. The battle there had been awful with many casualties on both sides. I was happy the Gettysburg boys of Company E missed out on that one.

Between Jack's letters and others in Gettysburg, the mothers and daughters and sisters and friends followed the war as best we could. Mrs. Skelly showed me the letters she had received. I filled her in on what Jack had told me. Mrs. Skelly certainly has it tough with a husband and a son at war. Young Daniel and Edwin were the only men she had at home anymore.

I also attempted to keep up the daily routine. I found it difficult not to wonder just where Jack and our boys were on any single day. Newspapers arrived after the fact. I knew in my heart that whatever I was reading about was not really where the war was on that particular day. I only knew that the war had been there recently and moved on. It was hard to tell exactly which ones involved our Gettysburg boys.

The Gettysburg boys returned home at the end of July, their enlistments being over. The town rejoiced. I was so happy to see Jack that I almost forgot to let go of my "welcome home" hug. The boys looked relieved to be home. We doted on them all. To us they were war heroes.

Jack and I spent a lot of time together, though I had to share him with his mother. He told me he was not comfortable being called a hero. He said they barely participated in the war and that certainly had made no noticeable contribution to the federal army.

I had an awful feeling that our time would be short and that before too long, he and the others would leave again.

My fears came to fruition in September when Jack, his brother Edwin, William Culp and other local boys joined up for three years. They were shipped back to York, Pennsylvania for camp.

I didn't think it was possible, but when Jack left this time, it was much harder than when he first enlisted or when he had been on furlough. Perhaps he had totally won my heart this time.

Nicholas Codori, one of Gettysburg soldiers, and Georgia's fiancé, Louis McClellan, chose to stay home. Jack had warned me that some would not sign up, but that they had completed the term they had enlisted up for. He encouraged me to support their decisions too.

When I saw them, I told Nicholas and Louis I was proud of their service.

Mother continued to encourage me to keep my focus on my chores and my brothers, as if not thinking about Jack and the others would keep me from worrying. For me it didn't work that way. The more I tried to put the Gettysburg boys out of my brain, the more they crept back in.

I tried to picture sleeping in a tent, marching along muddy roads, and even getting shot at. Even in my imagination, I could not know what the boys were going through.

My job as a seamstress, sewing for many of the neighbor ladies, involved many hours of my time on most days. Father had been gone so long that Georgia and I felt it our duty to give additional help to mother. Our working was making up for him not providing for us. Georgia and I were glad to bring in some money for the family and help mother purchase a house on Breckenridge Street.

Mother suggested years ago that we consider father dead, as she said he was a "good for nothing oaf." That was pretty hard for this girl to understand. I had prayed for several years every night that father would come home. But he never did.

As for me, I am rather outspoken. It was not something my mother liked about me. She came from a family where girls were to be "seen but not heard".

Around Jack Skelly, I was very bold. That surprised me. I guess that was because we have been together almost all our lives.

Jack was a follower, not a leader. He let Wesley Culp lead him around. Sometimes Wesley led him astray. If Wesley jumped off a bridge, I am sure Jack would follow without any questions at all.

I sometimes wished Jack would be more his own man, and not a Wesley Culp follower. I had just learned from his letter that Jack was now an officer. I thought perhaps now that Jack was a Corporal, he would learn how to lead.

My best subject in school was reading. I liked to read most anything. I think that started with my love for reading the Bible and expanded to other books.

Mother laughed when I told her I thought I wanted to be a teacher. She said I was not suited for that job. She thought my calling was to be a seamstress. I was good at that too. I just didn't think that was as important as the job of a teacher.

Jack thought I would be a good teacher. He said that because I taught him how to be a good kisser. He said I sure did a good job teaching him.

Georgia and I continued to support each other on a daily basis. She had been talking a lot with Salmone Culp, William's wife, trying to get some insight into what it was like to be married. Georgia and Louis had been planning their upcoming wedding. The Culps had been married for five or six years. Georgia passed information from Salmone on to me, so I would be ready when my day came too. I was beginning to think that would happen right after the war was over. And I was becoming more resigned that my station in life was to be Mrs. Jack Skelly.

Admittedly I didn't think that would be necessarily a bad thing. But I wondered. Was Jack the right one for me? Was he my only option? I wasn't getting any younger. And with all the men my age at war, there wasn't much hope around Gettysburg for me to see anyone else.

Life in Gettysburg was now all about coping. Some coped better than others. Mother had gotten along fine without father for many years, so other women looked to her for strength as they had to get along without their husbands and sons in recent times.

But since Louis didn't rejoin, Georgia spent much more time with Louis than she did with me.

I tried to live one day at a time. I stayed focused most times during the day on my work. It was at night that I got the most worrisome and the loneliest. I didn't think I could be like mother. I didn't think I could be on my own. I wanted the comfort of a life partner – someone like Jack. But I still wasn't sure if he was the right one for me to marry. And I didn't know how to resolve that little dilemma.

Part IV

Fall – Winter 1861 – 1862
John Wesley Culp

We have been at Camp Harmon near Centerville, Virginia since July. I worried often about my sisters Annie and Julie. I prayed for them each night. I wished that I could get a letter to them across the lines to let them know I was all right. But that wasn't possible.

John showed me his letters from his wife, Mary. They were the couple I boarded with in Shepherdstown. She was a faithful writer. He said he missed her terribly. I missed Mary probably as much as he did.

Before the war, often in the late evenin, when I couldn't sleep, I would walk quietly around their house where I stayed. Often I would find Mary sittin in the dark in her favorite chair, just starin out into the night.

At first I was not at ease comin upon her as we whispered so John would not hear. But before long, it was a part of the night I looked forward to.

Mary, though married, seemed to be a very lonely woman. She told me John was a wonderful man, but he could not provide comfort for her.

As the evenins continued, I found Mary to be a most wonderful woman. I got closer to her than any woman I had ever known. She told me of her fears and difficulties. Our times together were rare at first. Then they happened every single night.

The meetins were quite innocent at first too. It was two strangers gettin to know each other. I sat on the floor in front of her chair, keepin my distance. The cracklin of the fire on winter nights proved to be too noisy to talk – so we moved closer together.

As time went by and we got more at ease, Mary told me to sit close to her on the sofa. She laid her head on my lap as we talked. The closeness aroused me to the point that I worried that she would discover my manhood.

Our arms and hands bumped together every once in a while. And then as time went on, our touches became more and more planned.

We never kissed but we certainly comforted each other with gentle nudges and touches.

I think I provided her with some comfort. She said in listenin to what she had to say, I became a valuable friend to her.

By readin Mary's letters to John, it almost seemed that she was talkin to me. She often told him of things that she had told me. I felt she was writin those things for me, and usin John as the way to tell me somethin. I am sure that her letters gave me as much comfort as they gave John.

Our boys of Company B were involved in several picket actions near Munson Hill and Accotink Creek. There we watched the federal troops from a distance. I hoped they would come closer, but it never happened. I was not sure they knew we were nearby.

When I was on picket duty, on quiet nights, I could actually hear the federal boys talkin just a few yards away. But as long as they didn't bother me, I didn't bother them either.

Besides that, camp life was a dull and borin routine. I liked dull and borin compared to what we went through at the battle at Manassas Junction in July. I was willin to fight again, but not beggin to be sent into battle at this time.

On November 8, we were boarded onto rail cars at Manassas Junction. We were moved to the Shenandoah Valley. We arrived the next day in Strasburg. As soon as we unloaded off the train, we were ordered to march north to Winchester. Our quarters were set up at Camp Stephenson five miles north of town. We stayed through November and December.

Camp was cold and wet. We had learned in camp that it was important to keep our powder dry so our muskets could be fired when needed. The officers never said nothin about keepin our clothes and blankets dry.

Together the combination of cold and wet was most annoyin. Even when all my gear was dry, I did not like the cold. It was so cold some nights that the water froze in my canteen. The hair on my beard often had ice in it when we were marchin. A times I had to chip off the ice on my face. Wadin across a frozen stream on some march to nowhere kept me shiverin for hours.

The rain and snow combined to muddy the roads. The wet mud grabbed at my shoes when I tried to march. It was good we were not doin any fightin in the winter, cause I was in no mood for that.

We recently were introduced to a new recipe. It was called "lobskous". It sounded good when they said what we were havin. But it turned out to be just another attempt to disguise hardtack – this time they crunched hardtack, soaked it in water, and then fried it in pork fat. It was not my favorite meal in camp.

Company B's only action durin that time was an assignment led by General Jackson on December 17 to breach Dam #5 on the Potomac River near Hancock, Maryland. The dam fed water into the Chesapeake and Ohio Canal.

Our orders were to cut off the water to the canal, which was an important supply line for the federal army. Our mission was not as easy as we thought it might be. We stood in the icy water in the dark four nights in a row and hacked at the dam with axes and picks. For the entire time we were workin there, we could only make a small hole in the masonry dam. At times shots were sent our way from across the river. Mostly that was just a bother. It was certainly nothin like being in a battle. For that I was grateful.

Even if the mission was not a complete success, the soldiers of Company B were proud to have been a part of the duty. It beat the boredom of camp life.

One mornin near Hancock when our boys woke up, the ground was covered with about five inches of snow. Several still asleep looked like white logs. Men around the camp balled up the snow and threw it at anyone and everyone. It was quite a treat to actually have some fun.

Our orders on New Year's Day, 1862, were to move out. We marched a short way to Bath, Virginia and captured the town. That night we slept inside on the floor of a large room in the Berkeley Springs Hotel.

Then we marched to Romney, Virginia. The federal army had their way in Romney before we arrived, burnin many of the houses and leavin animals dead in the fields. One story I heard was that a lady begged the federal troops to allow her to take some valuables out of the house before they burned it. The federals let her to take an old clock and some bedding out onto the lawn. They burnt the house. And then the dirty rascals set the bedding and clock on fire too. The federals left town before we got there.

We were on the move almost every day, marchin through snow, sleet, rain and slush. I was cold and miserable. My uniform never dried out that whole time. My shoes and socks were always wet too. After we got back to camp, we heard reports that our discipline along the way was deemed good with our efficiency rated excellent. Perhaps we finally were becomin real soldiers.

When we marched back to Winchester on January 25, we were stationed at Camp Zollicoffer.

Within a few days after we arrived, a Jefferson County man, James Miller, from the 12th Virginia Cavalry, was scheduled to be executed by Lawson Botts' men. Miller had been charged with attemptin to murder his company commander. He was found guilty and sentenced to death.

Our whole regiment was required to watch his execution by the firin squad. Officers made us line up in rows on three sides of the area where the sentence was to be carried out. We stood at attention and watched as the man was brought to the enclosure. He was bound with rope, his hands tied behind his back. A grave had been dug and a coffin was lyin on the ground. Miller was made to sit on his coffin. A minister prayed with him. And then his eyes were covered with a bandana tied behind the back of his head. He was told to stand. He stood. At the command, twenty-one boys standin about ten feet from him fired their muskets all at once into his body.

The soldier dropped to the ground. Men placed him in the coffin and set him in the grave. They threw dirt on the coffin and patted down the earth. A small marker with his name was pounded into the ground.

No one in the lines said a word. And no one talked about it that night or the next. It was like it never happened.

I hated watchin the firin squad worse than I hated seein a solider shot in battle. It was just another ugly part of the war.

On March 9, we were told that the federals would be marchin again toward Winchester. We were ordered to Mt. Jackson. We marched forty-two miles south to get there. At dawn on March 22, we were headin north again, with our entire Stonewall Brigade marchin twenty-five miles to Cedar Creek. The following morning, March 23, we were up early again, in formation, makin our way another fourteen miles and arrivin at Kernstown at about two in the afternoon.

The 2nd Virginia Volunteer Infantry was missin Companies D, H and I as we prepared for action. Those three companies were with Turner Ashby and his horse artillery. We were sent into battle with orders to turn the federal army's right. General Jackson pushed the assault with information that the federals had just four regiments in the field.

We charged forward toward our target, a gang of federals hidin behind a stone wall. Fire from their battery kept us from reachin our destination. Only the right side of our line got to the wall.

Fightin was fierce. Men from both sides were fallin like hail. As for me, I kept goin through the nine steps and firin at the federals, hopin against all hope that my shootin was helping our boys out. Minie balls whizzed by me more than once, startlin me at first. Thank God none hit me.

Not too much later, the order was given to retire from the field. When we did, we counted the brigade's losses as six dead, thirty three wounded and fifty one missin in action. Company B had lost one dead, one mortally wounded and eight missin. The one man killed from our unit was John S. Feamon. He was the first from Company B to give his life in this here war.

Orderly Sgt. T. H. Towner, who was 40 years old and a veteran of the Mexican War, was mortally wounded in the battle. He was married to Mrs. Laura Parran of a very prominent family in Shepherdstown and was our postmaster. Towner was in charge of the records of Company B. He died several days later. With his death, the company's records were lost too.

Two recent casualties of our local boys came from the same family including William Fitzhugh Lee, the son-in-law of Mrs. Parran, who we lost at Manassas Junction.

Among those missin from Company B and assumed now to be federal prisoners were Jacob F. Voorhees, Samuel S. Hudson, Samuel P. Humrickhouse, Lemuel T. Taylor, Charles F. Ferrell, Selby M. Hamtramck, James P. Conly and Daniel M. Entler.

I heard after the fightin that information General Jackson was relyin on had caused him to misjudge the strength of the enemy forces. The federals actually had a whole division at Kernstown, outnumberin our boys with two federals to every one rebel soldier.

General Jackson was angry that the information he had been given was wrong. Two of the scouts were sent to the brig to let us all know how serious General Jackson was. The General demanded to receive correct information in the future.

General Thomas "Stonewall" Jackson

Fall – Winter 1861 – 1862
William Esaias Culp

On October 22 we were ordered on scouting patrol to Lutherville, Maryland. It was only four or five miles. The excursion was said to be a false alarm. We marched back that afternoon.

Several days later we marched to nearby Townsontown, Maryland and back.

At the end of October our orders were to march to meet with Colonel Dixon Miles and then to march back, a very short distance. When the march was short, we did not complain even though it seemed there was no reason for that particular march.

Upon arriving at Camp Buehler in Lutherville, Maryland, in early December 1861, it was our job to construct simple huts of logs to be our home through the winter.

My job was to lay the logs and notch them to fit together. Some of our boys of Company F either were cutting logs in the woods, digging out the foundation or pushing wet mud in the spaces between the logs. Other boys built a chimney in the one end or helped thatch a roof. When finished, we had a small two story hut to stay in. It wasn't fancy, but it was certainly adequate. It kept out some of the cold, snow and wind.

I wrote to my wife and sisters when the hut was finally finished. I told them that we were as comfortable in our new huts as anyone could be in anticipation of winter. I told them I was sorry I was still not able to send them money. I had been in the federal army since April and had not been paid the entire time. I let them know that I was not happy to be spending Christmas in Maryland, so close to home but so far away.

We got dried meat almost every day in camp. But because of the time of year, it was rare when we saw a vegetable or any kind of fruit.

Winter camp was cold, wet and boring. If it wasn't cold or wet, the wind was blowing so hard it was difficult to stand on sentry duty facing into the wind. But I couldn't turn my back on my duty either. It was those cold nights in winter camp that I thought about my decision to sign up again. Of course, it was becoming less and less likely that the war would be short, as many had earlier predicted.

Several of our men in Company F died during the winter camp including Edward Seitz, Forrest Little and Emanuel Wysotsky. Seitz and Little were reported to have camp fever.

Two others from Company F were missin and presumed to have deserted. They were William A. Klingle and Richard L. Cook. I was surprised that they deserted. If they had been caught, they would have been shot at a firing squad.

I continue to get encouragement from my letters from Annie and Salmon. Annie said the women of Gettysburg had foolishly thought their boys would be home by Christmas.

Salmone wished that I would be home for Christmas. This will be our first Christmas apart ever. I missed her greatly as my favorite holiday came and went. I told her in my letter that winter camp was at least far away from the war. For that I was most grateful this holiday season.

Some days our coffee froze in our cups before we got a chance to drink it. Some mornings my wet socks stood up by themselves because they were frozen too.

I had to share my letters with my friends, especially ones who didn't get any mail at all. I was happy that my sister and wife wrote me regularly.

When the early spring arrived, we harvested the first ramps that came up and boiled them in a large pot. The smell was awful for several days as the pot boiled. But the onion soup was tasty, warm and wonderful.

Jack Skelly and I talked one night about the news from Gettysburg. I told him I had heard several nasty things from William H. H. Pierce, a local lad. Jack wasn't surprised. Pierce's sister, Tillie Pierce Alleman, never had anything good to say about Jack's girlfriend, Jennie.

Fall – Winter 1861 – 1862
Johnston Hastings "Jack" Skelly Jr.

We entered winter camp at Lutherville, Maryland and spent the first weeks building huts to stay in. I am reminded of the huts I had read about that George Washington's men stayed in at Valley Forge and the harshness of the winter they had to endure.

We befriended a dog in camp and made him the mascot of Company F. We named him "F". We have trained him to carry a basket and retrieve small items for us. He stayed in our tent. Someone kidded William that when he ordered "F" around, "F" didn't seem to follow his orders very well. William became angry at the comment and a fight broke out. The contents of the table in the tent were knocked on the ground before order was restored.

I suggested later that it would be better if William held his anger for the rebel boys rather than fighting with those lads in his own company. He didn't take well to that suggestion either.

I received letters recently from mother and Jennie.

Mother told me that she has not received any letter recently from father. I thought perhaps no news was better than bad news. She also said that she got frequent visits from the other women of Gettysburg because they knew she was by herself with only the help of Daniel who works at the Fahnestock Store. She complained that her other son, Edwin, neglected his poor mother by not writing to her, and asked me to remind him to write. Edwin told me that because I was the writer, that I should include information about him in my letters to mother to get him off the hook.

Jennie's letter let me know that she continued to miss me. She said that she looked in on mother and Annie and Julia Culp, knowing they needed the most support. I wrote again to Jennie to tell her about camp and that I continued to miss her. I wanted her to know too that I was all right, healthy and safe. I said we had not seen an enemy soldier in many months. I joked that I was not sure I would even recognize one if he appeared.

When the pay master finally came along, he only made partial payments to us. At that same time, Philip Leonson from Gettysburg visited Jerome Martin at camp. Edwin and I gave Philip forty dollars for mother with a note telling her to get either gold or silver at the bank. We sent our dirty clothes home with Philip too.

Major Buehler also visited our camp. Captain Martin was doing a good job as his replacement though if we were voting, we would have voted to have Major Buehler back.

Edwin tried to get a furlough for Christmas to go home and visit mother. It was not approved. He did, however, get a pass to visit father's camp at the end of December.

Our winter camp was mostly about cold and heavy snow. It was so cold on several nights that the surgeon had to amputate fingers and toes due to frostbite. As boys from Pennsylvania, we were used to plenty of snow and cold. But we had never been camped outside in it before.

Captain Martin and our boys of Company F had a grand time on Christmas Day. The good citizens of Lutherville provided a scrumptious dinner for us.

On most days our main enemy was not the Johnny Rebs. It was illness, fatigue, lack of food, boredom, and extreme cold.

The bugler was the most powerful man in camp except for the officers. We rose in the morning to the bugle call. We drilled at the bugler's guard mount call. We ate when he gave the meal call. We bedded down to his lights out call.

When we pulled picket duty, it was twenty-four hours long. We all knew that it was the pickets who protected the army. I took picket duty very seriously. I was alert and vigilant. I was also lonely and hungry. Pickets were not allowed to build camp fires. So I was usually cold and hungry too. Often the boys of Company F would at least bring coffee to me. For that I was grateful. There was no sleeping on picket duty. You could be executed for failing to stay awake.

To relieve boredom, the boys of Company F often played cards. Poker was the game of choice. I wasn't very astute in playing, but it passed the time. Edwin was better at the game and won some money recently. We sent home some meat with a visitor to camp for mother. Her recent letter thanked us for the meat. She had been having a difficult time due to an attachment on her house for past taxes. Mother was due payment from renters and was finally able to pay the taxes she owed.

The one place in camp that I visited a couple of times was the sick list. Even though it got me out of drilling and marching, I would have gladly given up the stay in the hospital tent for most anything else. Sickness was hard to avoid. It grabbed some boys and didn't let them go. I believe our regiment has had more die from disease than from battles.

Rumors heard at camp were that we would soon be sent to Harpers Ferry, Virginia, Fortress Monroe, also in Virginia, to Baltimore or to Florida. Recently we received honors for being the best drilled company in all the Union's volunteer service. And I guess we should be. We were still being drilled almost seven hours every single day. And we were still complaining, because none of us had gotten our full pay.

On Washington's birthday in February, Company F and two others, Company A and K, were sent to Baltimore for a military review by Major General Dix and Brigadier General Duryea. About five thousand federal soldiers participated.

At the affair, a beautiful new eight foot by twelve foot silk flag for the 87th Pennsylvania was presented to Major Buehler. It was a sight to behold. We will carry it proudly where ever we go.

We received new clothes including one pair of pants, a shirt, two pair of drawers, a pair of stockings, and a hat with feathers.

Edwin and I were quite surprised to receive a letter from father in late March. He was at Madison Hill, Camp Wilson near Washington City. He told us that they had not been paid either. His rheumatism was bothering him fiercely during the winter months. He told us that we could visit him from Baltimore by train for a round trip fee of only 130 cents.

Fall - Winter 1861 – 1862
Mary Virginia Wade

What was most annoying to me about this awful war was that no one on either side, that I knew of, was interested in anything other than shooting the boys on the other side. If it were up to me, I think I would have had them pause by now to have some kind of peace conference to try to negotiate a settlement. But what do I know? I'm just a girl.

When I told my idea to Georgia, she thought I was on to something. She too found the idea of war to be not worthy of continuing.

Excepting for the fact that there were almost no boys or men between the ages of sixteen and forty five in Gettysburg any more, the routine of this small town had not changed that much. The war was a long way off. Our only connection was in reading the accounts in the newspaper and in the letters we received from our friends.

In a recent letter from Jack, I learned that he was well. He told me that the boys from Company F were wondering what President Lincoln thought about their unit being kept so far out of the war. Jack said he thought they could march and drill as easily in Gettysburg as in Cockeysville, Maryland where they were camped. He said he was comforted by my frequent letters and grateful that I looked in on both his mother and Daniel.

I answered by telling Jack that he and the others from Company F were always in my prayers. We all prayed for their safety and that they would soon be back home. What I didn't tell Jack was that I feared for his well-being and doubted that the war would end soon.

Georgia, my mother and I were gaining in reputation as being good with the needle and thread. Work came in regularly. The money kept food on the table. Mother put some away for the future and whatever that might bring.

Our whole family was active at the St. James Lutheran Church in Gettysburg. We attended services regularly. Everyone at the church was aware of the situation with my father. I think they kept a better eye on us because of mother being basically by herself.

I prayed fervently in church. But I also pray often at home or most any place I was. Somehow I figured that I didn't have to just pray in church. I was pretty sure God didn't much care where I was when I asked him to protect the Gettysburg boys and in particular, Jack Skelly.

My Bible was worn and torn. I had heard it said that it wasn't much use having a Bible if I didn't open it and read it. I read my Bible every single day. I keep it close by all the other times. It was a comforting book to me, especially in times like these.

Mother has always encouraged us girls to help others. We have taken in six year old Isaac Brinkerhoff as a boarder in our house. He is my responsibility. I take his care very seriously. Isaac is very bright. I enjoy teaching him. We are working on the alphabet as I try to teach him how to read. I know reading is a skill that every youngan should have because it opened the door to all learning.

I spent most of the rest of my time helping my mother.

I was still not sure about Jack Skelly. We had been friends forever. In fact, I had been told that Jack and his mother showed up with a pie she baked and they delivered to my house the day I was born. Jack insisted that he remembered seeing me wearing nothing but my bare skin. I blushed whenever he told the story, but hardly think a boy of two years old would remember that. At least I hoped not.

Growing up Jack and I played together in the woods, and in the streets around Gettysburg. Often we were alone, as we got older. We mostly sat and talked.

Once in a while we kissed. I liked that. Jack said we were practicing for the day when we got married. At first Jack was not a real good kisser. I patiently worked with him so that he was paying more attention to detail. The results were a pretty amazing transformation. I liked the kissing and the practicing much more than the actual thought that someday we would be married.

Mother even asked me one day if Jack had ever kissed me. I blushed and told her the truth. Yes, he had kissed me. She would have died if I had admitted that I had also kissed Jack back. And I even boldly initiated the kissing on more that one occasion. I certainly would never have told my mother I actually taught him kissing techniques.

Mother said to be careful cause kissing led to making babies. And she wanted none of that for this unwed daughter. Initially I was shocked at the possibilities. Then I became determined to be real careful that we didn't make a baby. So I stopped kissing Jack temporarily, with that threat hanging over my head. But I liked kissing so much, the kissing started back up again in earnest after just a short period of going without.

It wasn't that I didn't like Jack. He had been my best friend for as long as I can remember noticing boys. He was handsome and smart. There was some mischief about him that I kinda liked. Mother liked him too. She admired that he was respectful of her. I liked that he told me I was just as smart as he was. I thought I was, but most boys in town would never admit a girl was smart.

Jack was also my protector, my strength and my friend. Maybe he was destined to be my husband. That part I was not sure about.

Jack insisted that I was "his girl." He said that God brought us together to be together forever. After the war he wanted us to marry. At first I liked the idea. I promised to write him. He kept his promise to write regularly to me. I guess after a period of his being away and coming home, we will both know more of what we want our future to be like. I can get valuable information from my sister Georgia who will be married soon. She will be able to tell me what it is like to be a wife.

Meanwhile, my feelings are of loneliness right now. I am missing Jack more as the days go by.

Winter in Gettysburg was long and hard. I didn't much like the cold. I didn't much like the darkness. I didn't like the fact that vegetables we had stored for the winter were gone before Christmas. I didn't like having to carry firewood into the house to keep the fire going.

The only good things about winter were pitching balls of snow with my younger brothers and with Isaac Brinkerhoff and keeping warm by our fireplace.

Our spirits were raised at Christmas time when seven hundred soldiers from the 10th New York Cavalry were transferred to Gettysburg for duty.

Spring on the other hand was one of my favorite times. I love the spring flowers, the new blossoms on the trees, looking for my first robin of the year, pulling up those early ramps and making soup, and finally being able to get outside.

There were happy times in Gettysburg this spring. On April 15, 1862, my sister Georgia and John Louis McClellan were married at St. James Lutheran Church. My sister looked beautiful in the long white gown my mother and I had made for her.

As I watched them take their vows, I thought of Jack and myself. Was a wedding in our future too?

Mother let Georgia and Louis have her bedroom for their wedding night. She joined me in my bed. I got the side nearest the wall. At first I heard unusual noises in the night coming through the wall. I thought Louis was beating my sister. I almost pounded on the wall. I thought of running over to their room to protect my sister. I was confused. Finally it dawned on my little brain that Louis was not hitting her, he was loving her.

I was embarrassed to have been kept awake all night by those loving sounds of Georgia and Louis. I promise that I was not trying to listen. They were so loud I couldn't help myself, even by putting my pillow over my ears.

The next day they prepared to leave for the McClellan House down the street. I visited them often and asked lots of questions.

"One day of being Louis' wife was better than all the days that I have lived. To lay in his arms, and know that my future is with him as my husband, cured all the ills I have ever known." Georgia told me. She said she hoped someday that Jack and I would be married too.

I am always real honest when it came to talking to Georgia, but I could not bring myself to tell her that I had heard their loving on their wedding night.

In the weeks that followed, in Georgia's face, I saw happiness. I wanted that kind of happiness. Would that happen with Jack and me? I was frightened with the news in town, in the newspapers and in the letters I received from Jack. The war that people thought would end soon, had no end in sight.

How many of the Gettysburg boys would be left in an unmarked grave along the way? I feared for every one of them. I prayed for them all.

I read and re-read Jack's letters. I was still having my doubts about him and our future. But I continued to write to him. He said my letters brought comfort to his heart on days where there was little comfort at all.

Part V

Spring - Summer 1862
John Wesley Culp

We were camped at Winchester, Virginia, in late March of 1862. I am not quite sure what happened one fine evenin while we were there. John and I and about a dozen others from our unit were on furlough. We were comin back to camp after visitin the local watering hole. All of us had been drinkin some fine ale. Our men were talkin loudly. We were braggin about how brave our rebel boys were. It could be said we were not real keenly aware of what was happenin.

When we came up over a small hill just a few miles from camp, we were starin into the barrels of some pretty fine federal muskets. About twenty or so federal soldiers were only a few feet in front of us. Even a poor shooter could have killed us all. We raised our hands while at the same time lookin around. More federals were on either side and behind us. We surrendered our arms, droppin our muskets and held up our hands. That way, we figured, at least they wouldn't shoot us.

They took my prized gun, the one with the short stock so my finger could reach the trigger. They set us in line and marched us back toward the town. I talked to the federal boy walkin next to me and keepin me in line with the other prisoners, tryin to convince him that I was the only one in either army who could fire that musket with the sawed off stock. I told him that he should keep an eye on my special musket and give it back when we were exchanged. And that I would pay him handsomely to get my musket back. I promised not to ever fire it again at another Union soldier, which is what we would have to give as the oath anyway.

They marched us to the Winchester. Amongst the 2nd Virginia boys captured with me were my close friend, John, Jerry Sheffler, from the Hoffman Company in Shepherdstown, William H. H. Hawn, Jacob Hutson, George E. Adams, L.T. Rogers, Billie Butler, Benjamin F. Daniels, John B. Douglas, Thomas H. Wintermoyer, and Wells A. Feaman.

The yard in front of the Winchester courthouse had been made into a stockade. It wasn't much of a stockade. It was just a fenced in area. There were probably 300 of us rebel boys there. We could have all climbed over the fence at once as it was only about five feet high. The two dozen federal guards would not have known which ones of us to shoot. Most of our men would have been gone before anyone would have been able to catch us.

But there was no need to escape. We were goin to be exchanged in a couple of days. The food wasn't awful. The nights were not too cold. None of us were real happy to be in prison. But we were not desperate to leave either.

We were restin instead of marchin. Even bein in the stockade for several days was better than marchin another twenty-five miles each day. No one was shootin at us. Life was not too bad at all.

All the boys of the 2nd Virginia at the stockade laughed about our capture. We decided it would be awful to have to tell our families that instead of bein captured in a battle, we were caught leavin the tavern.

John thought we should have been more on guard instead of takin the night off. After all, a war was goin on. He said he did not think it was fair for the federals to sneak up and capture men who were already drunk.

I thought it could have been worse. They could have shot a bunch of drunken soldiers and no one would have ever known.

The people of Winchester came by to visit us. Often they brought water and food. I think if they had it their way, the people of Winchester would have put the Yankees in the stockade instead. The local folks did not seem very fond of the Union soldiers.

Whenever we had been mustered in, part of our instruction was that if we were ever captured, it was the policy signed by both the North and the South, prisoners would soon be exchange. After bein here three weeks, we were complainin to the guards. We thought the exchange might come within the first few days of our capture. And we were hopin our rebel lads would grab some Union soldiers so we could be traded soon.

June started with no exchange in sight. We were all just growin old at the stockade in Winchester. It wasn't that we weren't gettin good treatment. We were. We were gettin fed too. It was annoyin that no one was workin to exchange us.

Sometime in the middle of June, I was surprised to have a visitor. A guard came to find me. He asked me to step over to the side fence. There standin in his federal uniform was my brother, William. He was the last person I would have thought would come lookin for me.

I had not seen William since mother's funeral almost six years ago.

"How ya doin, Wesley?" he asked.

"I'm doin great, William," I said politely. "They are treatin me first rate. I am gettin fed every day from the Union cooks. And no one has tried to kill me in several months. I will be exchanged in a couple of days. It doesn't get any better than this."

As usual, William had all the answers. "Wesley, take the oath and come home to Gettysburg like a good little brother," he said in his most charmin manner. "The people back home will forget that you were a traitor if you come home now. All will be forgiven. You can join the 87th Pennsylvania and fight for Mr. Lincoln's army."

"Get lost, William," I said walkin away from the fence. "Tell Annie and Julia not to worry about me."

William hadn't changed none. He was still tryin to lord over me, decidin that I could not make a decision like this for

108

myself. I could tell he still disliked me. And at this point I did not like him none either.

"Get back over here, Wesley," he pleaded, like a boy who was not gettin his way.

I turned and walked slowly toward him. "Julia's visitin your friends in Shepherdstown," William added. Maybe he thought bringin up my sister's name would make me think of family and want to return to Gettysburg. He was wrong.

I told him where I stood on the matter. "You are wastin your time, big brother. I chose the side I wanted to fight on. We've been whippin up on you federals pretty regularly. I don't see that changin very soon. I'll take my chances with General Stonewall Jackson and these here men." With that I walked back over to where John, Jerry and all the others were sittin on the ground and I joined them. I told them what had happened.

John asked why my brother and I didn't get along. Here's what I told him. "William and I ain't nothing alike as brothers. We are as different as a pig and a cow (with him being the pig). I like to work until I am finished with something. To William, there's always another day. I like to be serious about work. He likes to do most anything other than work or study. He is a night person. I work best in the day time. Where William will fight at the drop of a hat, I would rather argue and fuss, only to resort to usin my fists when all else fails."

"He thinks he is always right," I said. "Sometimes he is, even though I hate to admit it. But he ain't right all the time. No one is right all the time. As for me, every once in a while I am right. But it seems in my case it is an accident when it happens. My brother's bigger than me, so I gotta either keep out of his way, and use my brain to outsmart him or my speed to outrun him."

I told them "William and I fought a lot back home. William had told me from those first moments that I didn't belong in this family. At first I believed him. After a while I ignored him. Mother said God wants us to love, not hate. William disliked me, but mother said I couldn't dislike him back. I had to love him. I didn't think that was fair, but I believed mother. I tried to like him, but ended up just not likin him very much. Even with that, William never accepted me."

Two days later I was told I had another visitor. When I walked to the fence I was surprised to find that it was the same one as before – my brother William.

William was smilin like we were old friends. I knew he was up to something. "I'm givin you one more chance to come home with me, Wesley," he said. "I will sign a note agreein to forget that you joined the rebel army. It will never be mentioned again. That is my promise. Take it or leave it. But if you leave it, there'll be no turnin back. Do we have a deal?"

I turned and walked away without sayin a word. I could hear someone screamin over at the fence. I was real darn sure it was William and that those screams were for me. I didn't look back. I was not interested at all in what he was peddlin. He had missed his chance years ago for me to pay attention to him and pretend to be his friend.

Six more weeks went by. The boys and I were angry cause there seemed to be no progress on our exchange. Week after week we asked, and as often as we asked, we were put off. Finally, we were told around the first of August that the exchange would be coming within a week. Of course, by that time, we tried not to get too excited, as we had been disappointed so many times before.

The exchange was finally set up. My dealins with the young guard at the Winchester stockade had paid off. My own private gun was with the items returned to me followin our oath. I thanked the guard with two silver coins.

All the Shepherdstown boys from the stockade walked back home, leaving Winchester on August 5. It was our intent to stop at home and stay for a few days. And then we would search for the 2nd Virginia soldiers. We had to hide out in Shepherdstown, because if anyone saw us, we might be turned in as deserters.

Mary greeted us with surprise and then joy. She hugged John lovingly and shook my hand.

Mary provided John and I with cover and delicious meals. I can not remember when I ate so well. I slept in my own bed too. That felt real good after what was more than a year of sleepin on the ground.

And in the evenins, when John was fast asleep, Mary and I began our nightly talks in the quiet of the parlor. We picked up about where we had left off before. But there was no shakin hands with me now.

Now the evenins with Mary seemed even more friendly than she had been in the past. She reached out and touched my face, tellin me that she had missed me greatly. It seemed to me that Mary was much happier to see me than she was to see John.

During the night, when we secretly met, she put her arms around me and held me tight. I could feel her heat through her nightshirt.

When I sat near her on the sofa, she motioned for me to go down to the floor. She joined me there, pullin me close so that we lay together side by side.

Now there was no hidin my aroused state. She straddled my body and lay on top, kissin me passionately. I never wanted to let her go.

Mary drew me a bath one day while John was sneakin out lookin for war news. And she was not shy about watchin me get out of the tub. She held a large towel and very slowly helped me dry off. I was likin Mary more and more.

John and I talked about needin to find our boys of the 2nd Virginia Volunteer Infantry. He said several of the boys from the stockade had already left to catch up with them. As for us, we hadn't decided what we were goin to do. As for me, I personally wasn't real excited about rejoinin our regiment.

Union Stockade at Frederick County Courthouse
Winchester, Virginia
From James E. Taylor's Sketchbook
The Western Reserve Historical Society
Cleveland, Ohio

Spring - Summer 1862
William Esaias Culp

We were camped at Point of Rocks in Maryland, along the Potomac River near Harpers Ferry.

I don't know what got into me. As soon as I heard my brother was in the stockade at Winchester, Virginia, I felt that I needed to visit him. I got a pass and went to the stockade, which was located on the front lawn of the Frederick County Courthouse in Winchester.

I asked to see the littlest soldier they had captured. They knew who I wanted to talk to. I had no problem seeing him. It didn't seem like such an awful place.

Wesley was as stubborn as a mule. He hadn't changed much at all. I suggested he come home and fight for Mr. Lincoln's army. Somehow that suggestion seemed an insult to him. He didn't like it none that I called him a traitor either.

He never could get anything right – and his choice to fight with the rebels was in tune with all his other bad decisions. He will live to regret it or perhaps die to regret it. I am certain we will win this war.

I thought maybe I should stick to fighting. Talking didn't get me anywhere with Wesley. Next time I will shoot at Wesley instead of trying to talk some sense in him.

Mostly the boys from the 87th Pennsylvania were brave, honorable and reliable. But in the spring and early summer five of the Gettysburg boys of Company F were found missing and were believed to have deserted. They were Gerald W. Ford, Joseph Houck, Jacob Dearddorff, John Wallech, and George Markle. We never heard from them again. Deserters if caught would have been sentenced to death by firing squad. It shook the resolve of those of us who stayed. Desertion for most of us was not something we would have ever considered.

Conrad Gerecht of Company F was so sick he was given a medical discharge and was sent home.

The 87th Pennsylvania Company F left Point of Rocks on June 1, 1862 and marched along the Baltimore and Ohio Railroad to Edward's Ferry which was downstream from Leesburg, Virginia. We participated in the destruction of about twenty boats on the Potomac River. Our mission accomplished, we marched back to Point of Rocks. We camped for three more nights before marching to Frederick Junction in Maryland. There we boarded a train and were taken to Baltimore where we set up camp at Camp McKim.

I received a letter from my sister Annie. I wrote to her from camp to tell her that I had visited Wesley in Winchester at the federal stockade. I informed her that he was well but still stubborn and a traitor. I didn't tell her that Wesley pretty much ignored my attempt to help him enlist in the federal army with the rest of us.

A letter from Salmone had also arrived in camp. I answered her, telling her too of my visit to Wesley. Salmone knew how I felt about Wesley, so I filled her in with more details than I had shared with Annie. I dearly missed my beloved wife, Salmone.

After being in Baltimore for nearly two weeks, we received new orders. We boarded the Baltimore and Ohio Railroad train again on June 23 and were sent to Camp Jessie at New Creek in far western Virginia. Thirty six boys seemed not ready for any action, deserted the night before we moved out.

Our new assignment was about 200 miles from Baltimore. We thought this might mean that finally we would see some fighting that we had been trained for. The new place was desolate, with high mountains, and roads that were rough and hard for marching. We camped near the river, only to have severe thunderstorms threaten to wash away everything we had.

I wrote to Salmone and my sister to acknowledge where I was now camped. I offered that we were to guard the railroads, a task some of the 87th Pennsylvania boys had done before in Pennsylvania and Maryland. I told them how grateful we were that they transported us 200 miles from Baltimore by cars, rather than having us march here.

It took us until August 21 to actually get close to finding the rebels we were supposed to be engaging. Even then a battle was avoided.

Toward the end of August, Major Buehler told us he was leaving our command to become a colonel in a newly organized draft militia. He was going to stay with us until the first of December when the new regiment was formed. When he told us, many of us were unhappy with his decision. Some thought in a sense that he had trained us and then would be deserting us.

We marched to Clarksburg, Virginia on August 28 and then marched three different times to Beverly and back.

We marched back and forth and all around from our arrival at the camp until the end of August without seeing any rebels at all. We waded the Cheat River four separate times, going back and forth, across one day and then back several days later. It was said by someone from the 87th Pennsylvania that one mile here seemed twice as long as one mile back home in Pennsylvania. That was because of the rough terrain and thick brush that stood in our way. We had barely enough to eat on any given day. It was also about two times hotter than Baltimore. The sun blackened our skin.

Our orders included keeping General Ewell's men from plundering the military stores along the tracks. Our boys were spread for thirty miles all along the rail lines.

Guarding the bridges was easy duty, but was about as far away from the actual war than anyone could be. The only real enemies any of us saw during this duty were mosquitoes bigger than wrens and yellow jackets. As far as I know, we suffered no casualties on railroad duty.

I was sure standing guard of the railroad bridges was important duty. Someone had to do it. But this wasn't exactly what I had in mind when I enlisted.

Half of us stood guard duty one night and the others relieved us and stood guard the next night. The duty was sheer boredom. I never saw a rebel soldier the whole time I was there. Only once did we get near a rebel. That was when a boy from York was shot in the leg while on patrol.

We had nine hundred boys. Not all were ready to see action because typhoid fever had taken a toll. Our colored regimental cook Butler died in July. Privates Joseph Wysotsky, Basil Little and Michael Crilly were sent to the hospital in Wheeling, Virginia. Crilly was sent home with an honorable medical discharge. The two others were returned to the regiment.

It was my thought that the government sent us to an outpost as far away from the action as they possibly could. And I was not sure why. We didn't know where the war was, but we knew we were not part of it.

Certainly we were a trained fighting force. But we were quite far away from any action. Perhaps that had something to do with the fact that the payroll office still had not listed us for pay. The boys were terribly cross about not getting paid. It looked to us like Washington had decided the 87th Pennsylvania didn't really exist as a regiment. That way they didn't have to pay us. So they shipped us out into the frontier where we couldn't get our names in the newspaper for being in any battle. And we would be too far from Washington to send someone from the regiment there to harass them about the money we were owed.

We were pretty much lost in the western Virginia woods. Even the darn rebels couldn't find us.

Spring - Summer 1862
Johnston Hastings "Jack" Skelly Jr.

Brigadier General Cooper reviewed our regiment at Camp Buehler on April 17. General Cooper had been an attorney in Gettysburg and a man most of us had known for a long time. We were complimented again for our drill proficiency, our fine soldiering and the appearance of our men.

Mother's latest letter and package arrived at the end of April. The package included mince pies, cakes, eggs and butter for my brother and I for Easter. We were grateful.

She told me several things I had not known. She said Wesley Culp had been taken prisoner and was in a stockade in Winchester, Virginia. An exchange was supposed to take place soon. She had received a letter from father and thought he might be close to doing battle near Yorktown, Virginia. Mother feared more for his safety, I think, because of his age than she worried about my brother and me.

My return letter thanked her for the package. It was delivered pretty much intact from Mr. Myers who was here to visit his son. I assured mother that both Edwin and I were healthy and making it through.

Two letters from Jennie arrived at the end of the month. She too had information about Wesley's stay in the stockade which she got from Annie. Jennie said she felt sympathetic to Annie for all her burdens, not the least of which was raising her sister, Julia, with no help at all. Jennie said that her sister and she helped their mother with the sewing and were making some extra money doing that.

On May 16 we marched to Townsontown, Maryland for a dress parade and drill. Our regiment band held a concert. The local people received us with great excitement.

Recently I made some extra money fixing musket straps and altering uniforms and sent fifteen dollars home to mother and ten to Jennie.

Edwin surprised me today by announcing to Company F that he was marrying Miss Sue Craver from Creagerstown, Maryland when the war was over. He had been engaged to her for over a year. He said he had recently told mother in a letter and was awaiting her approval. I think mother will be surprised but happy for him.

I suggested perhaps we could have a double wedding to include Jennie and myself. He said he was open to that suggestion, but needed to talk to Sue.

Daniel wrote to us at the end of May. He was interested in our regimental dog and wondered if we could steal a good rat terrier for him. He told us that he was taking care of mother as best he could when he was not working at the store. He appreciated the razor strap we had sent him.

In early June, we were ordered to Point of Rocks, Maryland, for temporary assignment.

Word from William was that he had visited Wesley in the stockade made me smile. I knew William well enough to know he probably insulted Wesley. William was the kind of lad who would think nothing of berating Wesley for his decision to become a rebel soldier. William was real annoyed that his brother was fighting for the enemy.

I was pretty sure William had made a scene and left in a huff. I was just as certain that Wesley wasn't willing at that point to give William the time of day. Wesley was smart enough to fend for himself.

Wesley knew William had an agenda – to let everyone know that William was always right. Of course, Wesley and I knew that wasn't possible. Wesley's joining the southern army didn't affect what I thought of him. Wesley Culp was still my best friend.

We rode back to Baltimore on the Baltimore and Ohio Railroad in mid-June for a dress parade. First Lt. James Adair commanded Company F in place of Captain Martin who had resigned. The boys of the company were not told the captain's reason for resigning and we were angry about that.

With Captain Martin leaving, there were rumors in camp that our regiment would be divided up. It was said that we would be sent to guard various hospitals. We all hated those possibilities. We wanted to stay together. The boys were angry for several days until our orders came through. We were going to be sent to New Creek, Virginia. Our company was happy we would all go together to New Creek which we were told was about 15 miles beyond Cumberland, Maryland.

When we arrived, I let mother know that we were now camped in the hinterlands of far western Virginia about 200 miles for Baltimore. I told her that there would be no more package deliveries, because no one, including the enemy and the paymaster, was likely to be able to find us. I wondered to her why the President was so interested in having us protect the railroad here, but not interested in having us participate in the actual war.

My letter to Jennie informed her of my new location, somewhere in the middle of nowhere. She would appreciate at least that I was under no enemy fire and thus safe and sound. I explained that I doubt if anyone, including our paymaster or the rebel army, would be able to find us now.

We fell into a dull routine. We participated in marching back and forth, for no apparent reason at all. I complained to the lads in my tent in the evenings. All were sympathetic. I wondered out loud just how we were contributing to saving the Union as we were now in the far western portion of Virginia, far away from any of the rebel army. No one in Company F seemed to be able to answer my questions.

I even asked "Was I just complaining for no reason?"

"No," they agreed. "You certainly have reason to ask the questions. We just don't have any answers."

I also remembered that General Patterson had once told us that we weren't supposed to think. We were just to follow orders. And that's what we did.

It even occurred to me that Lt. Adair probably didn't know why we were ordered to this God forsaken area and then ordered to march here and there and over yonder way.

This had not been the best of times for me. Seems like I had gotten every dreaded disease that had visited our camp. I had no desire to eat, cause whatever I ate came up again or went through me. I was too weak on most days to lift up from my cot.

At first they thought I had typhoid fever. Some of the other boys already had been diagnosed as having it. They separated me even from the others in the hospital tent. But I was lucky. I did not have typhoid fever. But I definitely had diarrhea. I would rate diarrhea the worst ailment of all. I have had it so bad that I have asked God several times to let me die. Some in our regiment have already died of diseases including diarrhea.

Just in the last few days I have finally been able to keep my food from coming back up. I feel much improved over last week's conditions. At least the blisters on my feet are healing cause I am not able to march.

Others were not so fortunate. Our colored cook, Butler, died from typhoid and several others were sent to the hospital in Wheeling, Virginia. Michael Crilly was medically discharged and sent back home by cars to Gettysburg.

I wrote to my brother Daniel in the middle of August. I told him of our routine here in the western outreaches of Virginia. I told him of all my ailments, but said I was much better now, as I didn't want mother to worry. I was sure Daniel would smile when I told him that our baggage was left in Harpers Ferry by mistake and did not arrive at our new camp.

My letter to mother informed her that Edwin and I were doing better, now that the doctor lacerated my tongue and that I was able to take nourishment. I told her that I was still weak and unable to drill and march, but that some fresh peaches and lemons had arrived from Cumberland and that they were wonderful to eat.

In Jennie's letter I let her know that I had been pretty ill, but recovering. I told her that my disposition had been vile due to lack of food, but that it didn't keep me from thinking kind thoughts of her.

It took me quite a while to get back on my feet after all my illnesses. I don't know which I hated more – the visit by diarrhea or the treatment which was a cup of castor oil and a tincture of iron three times a day. Either way, I was hoping to never, ever visit the sick tent again.

We can't much help it when we get sick. We all live in close quarters. If someone was sick, every one around him was probably going get that same illness. When you got sick, they sent you to the hospital where every darn boy there has some illness too. Its almost like if you give me what you have, I'll give you what I have. No one was likely to get back to camp real soon once they arrived at the sick tent.

When I got diarrhea, I thought the medics were plumb crazy. Everything they put in me ran right straight through me. Their solution was to give me liquids. I don't have a medical background in the least, but I didn't think that was the right solution. But a funny thing happened. Their remedy worked. And to think all I had wanted to do was die on that cot because the diarrhea had such an awful grip on me.

One hundred and twenty men at our camp each day dug fortifications. The 23rd Illinois joined us here at Camp Jessie. We were saddened that Jonathan Barnitz of York died this week. His body was sent back home on the Baltimore and Ohio Railroad.

On August 22, Company F left for Rowlesburg at 3 o'clock in the afternoon. We marched for a long time, stopping in the dark and rain to sleep on the ground. The next morning we crossed the Cheat River. It was so clear we could see speckled trout swimming in the river.

The next day, our destination was St. George's Court-house where we were to encounter 1,500 rebel soldiers belonging to Imboden's regiment. We were as excited as we had been since crossing over into the South over a year ago cause we thought we might finally get to shoot at some real rebel boys. Our regiment arrived at St. George's Courthouse, expecting a tussle, but we were again disappointed. The rebels had already left town.

Our orders came to leave New Creek on August 22. Lt. Norris was seriously ill. He was seen by the surgeon, Dr. McCurdy, and left at camp.

We evacuated Fort Elkerater with orders to destroy everything we couldn't take with us. Our orders were to march to Beverly at 11 o'clock. We marched all night and arrived at 8 o'clock the next morning. We rested until 5 o'clock, and then marched off to camp at the foot of Sand Ridge Mountain. The next day we marched to Phillipi. The following day we marched to Webster arriving at noon. Our boys had marched almost 186 miles since Rowlesburg.

Spring – Summer 1862
Mary Virginia Wade

Word around town had it that Wesley Culp had been captured in Winchester and was being held in the stockade at the courthouse. I asked his sister, Annie, if it were possible that Wesley had actually been captured. She said it was true. She said William had visited him and reported that Wesley was being treated well. Word was he would be exchanged soon.

At least I knew for sure where Wesley Culp was and that he was safe. I had no such information on Jack or any of the other Gettysburg boys.

On May 1 my letter to Jack announced that Georgia and Louis were married last week. I told him Louis and Georgia had moved into a house in the neighborhood and that I miss her already. I let him know that I would be visiting her often. I asked that he continue to be careful, as I feared every day for his safety.

His return letter told of his recent illness. I had read somewhere that illness was taking more soldiers than fighting in battles. I had not known that, and thus now had new worries. He claimed that he was far away from the enemy somewhere in far western Virginia.

June in Gettysburg marked the beginning of summer. It often also meant oppressive heat. And this summer was no different. The sun beat down on us. The town streets were more dust piles than roads. We welcomed an occasional storm to cool the air, water the crops, and hold down the dust.

A newspaper article I read in the *The Adams Sentinel* June 3, 1862 newspaper confirmed the information from Anne about her brother. The article said: "…our young townsmen, Wesley Culp, was taken prisoner in the battle of

Winchester – took the oath of allegiance to the United States – was released – then joined a band of guerillas."

The people of the town had accepted that our boys were not coming home soon. We were disappointed. But there was nothing we could do but try to make it through each day. We had learned by now to do the best we could under the circumstances.

I continued to read the war news in the newspapers. The news was depressing every single day. I wanted to live my life with optimism. There was no optimism in the war reports except for the fact that there seemed to be no recent battles involving the 87th Pennsylvania boys. We were frustrated though, never knowing which of our boys at any moment could be taken from us by enemy cannon, musket fire or disease.

The women of Gettysburg tried to be strong. My mother was someone the other women sought encouragement from. Most days Georgia and I marveled at mother's ability to remain like a rock.

The borough of Gettysburg limped along as best it could without its regular menfolk. Having the New York Cavalry stationed here at least made us feel safe and secure. Stores remained open but commerce slowed to a crawl. One of the highlights of my day was when the mail arrived.

Women seemed more likely to repair their old clothes than purchase anything new. Georgia and I could barely keep up with the demand for us to sew and repair clothes. The extra money made the longer hours worth the effort.

Fear of the unknown stepped ahead of rebel soldiers on our list of worries.

The local newspapers carried correspondence from the boys of Company F, 87th Pennsylvania. The *Gettysburg Compiler, The Star and Banner* and *The Adams Sentinel* seemed to be competing to see which one could offer the most up-to-date detail of the crisis.

Each day my brothers got closer to the age that they too would be going to enlist. Mother, Georgia and I never discussed that impending doomsday. It was horrific enough that Jack was gone. I was not sure mother could survive the call to war reaching her darling sons.

Georgia seemed to be really happy being Mrs. Louis McClellen. We talked about it often as I was curious. I was a tad jealous of the time she spent with him that she had shared with me before they were married.

My recent letter to Jack mentioned that the women of Gettysburg had recently secured a map to find where on God's green earth western Virginia actually was. It was comforting to notice that none of the battles discussed in the newspapers were anywhere's near where the 87th Pennsylvanians called their camp. I told Jack I thought he was in a pretty safe place.

I had always thought in a marriage the man was the stronger one of the two. And that women relied on their men when times got tough. But my mother had no man to lean on. My father had been gone since I was about seven years old. Mother was all by herself. Yet she seemed to not need anyone else. She relied on some inner strength that I admired greatly.

For me personally I leaned on my mother. But eventually, I wanted a man to guard and protect me, and to be strong when I was weak. I wanted someone to hold and comfort me when I was afraid. I was afraid today for the Gettysburg boys but had no one to comfort and hold me.

In the middle of August, Georgia and I went to visit Michael Crilly who had returned home from the front on a medical discharge. We visited in hopes of finding out about Jack and the other boys of Company F from someone who had been with them since April 1861.

Michael lay on the couch, drifting in and out of sleep. He looked awfully pale. I was not privy to what ailed him to the extent that he would be sent home to recuperate. We waited patiently to talk to him.

When he was alert, Crilly told us of all the hardships, especially those of the current location of the 87th Pennsylvania in far western Virginia mountains. He reported that Jack was doing as well as anyone, though he fought recent diseases that overtook the camp regularly. He said William Culp, Edwin and the others were also in good shape.

Disease, he explained, was a much more feared enemy than the elusive rebels who they had not seen in recent months.

When Crilly fell asleep talking to us, we took that as a sign to leave. Georgia and I were saddened by his state of health, wondering aloud if he would ever be himself again. He was certainly less of a boy than he had been when we knew him before his enlistment. We wondered how many others would return diminished, diseased, wounded or in pine boxes.

At least Crilly was home with his family to support him and not off somewhere getting shot at.

Mother continued to visit the homes of all the local Gettysburg boys who were away at war. She brought strength to those who were here at the home front trying to carry on. I marveled at her ability to portray the strong woman who had been missing her man far longer than any of the Gettysburg ladies. I am hoping someday I would realize that I had inherited some of that resolve from mother.

Part VI

Fall – Winter - Spring 1862 - 1863
John Wesley Culp

John and I talked about what we should do about our company and the war. He heard that General Robert E. Lee and the Army of Northern Virginia had crossed the Potomac River and invaded Maryland. We were quite excited about that news. John said the rebel army was in Frederick, Maryland. He said if we would walk toward Frederick, perhaps we could help General Lee.

On September 16, we crossed the Potomac River at Blackford's Ford near Shepherdstown and into Maryland. The ford was at the cement mill just below the dam. I was surprised to see the mill had been burned to the ground. There were only ruins of the mill where Congressman Boteler, who lived at Fountain Rock in Shepherdstown, had proudly produced cement to build the United States Capitol in Washington City.

The day was wet from the rain, so there was no dryin off from our fordin the river. Just to our left, but too far up the river for us to see, were the remains of the wooden bridge we had burned with Henry Kyd Douglas in our early days with the 2nd Virginia Infantry.

By the time we reached Sharpsburg, the little town was full of Confederate soldiers. General Lee's army was there preparin to fight.

I asked if the 2nd Virginia boys were there. I told the officer on duty that we had just been exchanged from prison in Winchester. We were lookin for our unit.

He told me the 2nd Virginia had not arrived, but that the Stonewall Brigade was here. We were sent to join them.

John and I found the Stonewall Brigade camped behind a small white church along the Hagerstown Turnpike. When we reached the camp, I asked to talk to an officer. He listened as I told him our story. He said he would be happy to have two veterans join the fight with his men.

John and I grabbed some vittles and some cold coffee. We found a place to sit. We rested on our arms, ready to head out at the time we were called.

Everyone around us was too excited to sleep. The officers talked about a major battle takin place the next mornin. There were no camp fires as the enemy was close by. We were given eighty rounds of ammunition each.

The boys around us were whisperin. They attached paper to their shirts with their names so if they didn't make it, someone would know who they were. Others asked the boys next to them to notify their folks if they were killed. John and I agreed to do the same. It was a little frightenin to do that, thinkin there might be no more days after tomorrow. There was no jokin like we normally heard at night in camp. Some boys were prayin out loud.

I wondered how many around us would act cowardly tomorrow, and do what we called the "cannon quickstep" – runnin the opposite way of the battle when the fighin got heavy around them.

I feared bein wounded and left on the field more than takin a direct hit that would kill me. I preferred to go right away and not have the pain linger. But my best idear was to make it through and to return to work and prosper when the war was over.

While it was still dark, the cannons started firin. The shot from the batteries shook the ground all around us. We could see the light flashin in the dark but couldn't tell what they were aimin at or if they were firin at our boys. The noise sounded like thunder.

As the sun rose on September 17, I could hear soldiers marchin down the road in the fog. The fog hid them from our sight and hid our camp from them.

Our men lined up quietly in battle formation. We waited. The day was already hot, even though it was just sunup.

I watched a cavalry soldier near our brigade tryin to calm his horse so he could mount. A cannon ball hit his horse, blowin the animal to pieces, and spillin blood all over the soldier. His right arm had also taken the ball, and his arm was hangin by a thread off his shoulder. He fell to the ground probably havin taken a mortal hit.

That was the worst hit I had even seen in my limited action in the war. It was horrible. I felt sick but knew I had to put that out of my head.

The fightin we were waitin for had begun. Cannons started firin at our position and fallin harmlessly behind our lines. We held our ground. The cannons kept firin. The shot got closer and closer to us. The noise was deafenin. It was strange but for some reason, I was calm and not afraid.

We moved out. The Stonewall Brigade was ordered into a double quick step. A cornfield lay directly in front of us. From the cornfield, a fierce musket fire smashed our lines, with men droppin all around John and myself. We gave them the old rebel yell, chargin ahead, firin back, over and over again. I was not sure eighty cartridges this day was goin to get the job done. The smoke was so think I could barely see. We were in an awful scrape. I was not sure any of us would live to see tomorrow.

Our brigade held our ground, charged ahead briefly, and then fell back. I had never seen so many federals in one place. They were everywhere. There were more of them than I had ever seen, even at Bull Run.

Cannon fire shook the earth almost every single minute. I was hopin that at least half that fire was from rebel guns located behind us.

There was no time to think. All I could do was keep firin as long as I had cartridges. John stayed by my side. We had been in scrapes before, but nothin quite like this. No matter how many dropped from our fire, the enemy kept comin over the hill in waves.

More minie balls passed closer to me than ever since the war had begun. I was determined to fight as hard as I could. We had to step around soldiers layin and dyin on the ground. Many were real still and probably dead.

Officers shouted orders. The men of the Stonewall Brigade fought as valiantly as we had fought at Bull Run.

I was blinded for an instant by all the smoke. I coughed. When I looked up all I could see were federal soldiers in front, bearin down at us with their bayonets ready to run us through. The boys around me threw down their muskets and held their hands up high. They surrendered. John and I got the message and followed their lead. We surrendered too.

Our boys were rounded up with about 500 other rebel soldiers. At the end of the day, they marched us to Frederick, Maryland. There we were packed into train box cars like cattle and taken to Baltimore. They marched us to the Union prison at Fort McHenry.

Once again I bribed a guard to look after my musket. I had to convince him with three coins that the weapon was useless to anyone but a man of my size with a very short arm. I prayed it would be handed back when we were exchanged.

We were told that this was a famous fort now turned into a holdin pen for rebel prisoners. Francis Scott Key wrote the Star Spangled Banner here durin the shellin of the port of Baltimore in some other war.

Fort McHenry was a much different stockade than where we were held in Winchester. These lads here were serious. The stockade was a fortress in the Baltimore harbor with high stone walls closing us in. We couldn't even see over them. Guards walked on the tops of the walls and looked down at us. There were no friendly neighbors talkin to us and passin food and drink through the fence like before in the stockade in Winchester.

There was an unusual mix of prisoners here. In Winchester we were just among other rebel soldiers. Here we were told there were political prisoners includin Marylanders suspected of supportin the southern cause, and even some citizens like the mayor of Baltimore, the marshal of the Baltimore Police, a former Governor of Maryland, several members of the state government and even a few newspaper editors.

Us rebel boys were not unhappy to be here cause we were due to be exchanged rather soon. But those other fellows were madder than all get out, cause they were not goin nowhere. Those important political prisoners were kept separate and away from us. That was fine by me. I think there were maybe 300 rebel boys with free run of the large stockade.

Fort McHenry was not what I would call a picnic. We were each given a blanket but nothin else. We did get fed every day. Old Jefferson Davis never provided that much food for our army.

The meals were not much – breakfast was hardtack and coffee. Dinner was bean soup and hardtack. Supper was coffee, some kind of meat, usually salted pork or pickled beef, and of course, hardtack. I think they must have got a shipload of hardtack beins that the fort was right by the harbor.

Suttlers came into the stockade once a week and sold items to prisoners who had money. I was one of them. I bought tobacco and fresh fruit for John and myself and some honey for our coffee.

When we were not exchanged within a few days, I asked about it. I was told that the exchange was being discussed by both sides and a rulin would come down in the next month or so.

John and I settled into prison life for the second time in recent memory.

Several other prisoners told me that a guard at the main gate, who was only there certain nights, could be bribed. He liked silver coins. They said he let them out to go to the nearby tavern one night for a coin cause they had promised to come back before sunrise.

Of course John and I didn't believe a word of it. Next time they left, our new friends took us with them. And true to their word, the guard collected our coins and a promise to return. Said he'd track us down and kill us if we didn't come back by the time the sun came up. We paid up and promised.

We stumbled forward in the dark, followin our friend who said he remembered the way. We came upon a small tavern and entered.

We ordered a round of ales and found a table in the back. A busty lass brought our brews. No one seemed to notice our tattered uniforms, or at least they didn't seem to much care. The place was loud. Many of the men there were already quite drunk.

Several barflies lit on our table. One lad asked, "You're new around here, ain't ya?"

John gulped his brew and answered for all of us "Just passin through. Don't need no trouble."

The stranger asked, "Seen any action in the war?"

"In Virginia at Winchester and at Manassas and Sharpsburg, Maryland. That last one was bloody awful. On furlough for a few days now," John explained.

"This little runt a soldier too?" he asked, pointing directly at me.

John was quick, knowin I was big enough to stick up for myself, but probably not wantin me to bloody the lad's nose in this place. "That's my little brother. Yea, he's a soldier too. Don't get him riled up – he fights bigger than you might think."

"Meant nothin at all by it, lad," the drunk insisted, backin away from our table as he talked. "Think I'll be goin now. Good day lads."

I thanked John for stickin up for me. We drank two more rounds and bellowed out some tunes with the others. When it started to get louder and more rowdy, we slowly walked out so that no one would notice.

Findin our way back to the stockade was a bit of a problem. Our leader was not so sure of the direction. I'm thinkin it might have been smart to leave a trail of bread crumbs so we could find our way. Our friend had a few too many ales. The brews were gettin in the way of his sense of direction. When we finally arrived back, the guard seemed relieved that we had returned. "Welcome back to the Baltimore Bastille," he said. I am guessin he would have been in trouble if the count came up four prisoners short on his watch.

In the middle of October, we were told we had to sign an oath of allegiance to the Union to be givin our freedom. John said he was not sure what to do. He had not felt honorable signin the oath at Winchester, knowin full well that we would shoulder our arms against the Union within a month of our promise.

John wrote to Mary to ask her wisdom on the matter. He insisted that she could offer me good advice too.

Here's what John wrote:

Fort McHenry, Maryland
October 5, 1862

My wife, Mary

Wesley and I are prisoners here. We were captured in Sharpsburg, Maryland. We are being treated well.

I need to ask you something. As a privilege of parole, if we pledge an oath to never take up arms against the Union, we will be released. Wesley and I will be able to come home to Shepherdstown.

Your advice on this matter will be taken as gospel.

We anxiously await your reply.

Love,

Your husband, John

In early November, Mary's letter arrived. Inside John's envelope was a sealed letter addressed to me.

John shared his letter with me. I lied to him about my letter. I was not willin to tell him what Mary had suggested that I do.

Here's what John's letter said.

Shepherdstown, Virginia
October 25, 1862
Dear John
You were born in the South. You have lived in the South throughout your whole life. Swearing to that oath would be living a lie. Rot in prison, but don't sign the oath.
Your wife
Mary

The letter that I did not let John read, Mary's letter to me, was very different. Here is her letter to me.

Shepherdstown, Virginia
October 25, 1862
Dear Wesley
You were born in the North. You have family in the North. Swear the oath, kiss the book and hurry on home.
Mary

I left the next mornin after signin the oath. The guard returned my trusty musket to me and I paid him well. I did not wish to see John before I left. I do not know what happened to him.

It took me most of a week to walk and grab occasional rides on farm wagons to travel about ninety miles back to Shepherdstown. I was stopped several times, but was carryin papers, so most everyone left me alone. Besides, bein so small, most probably thought I was just a lad with a pretend gun tryin to look like a real soldier.

Mary seemed real happy to see me. She wrapped her arms around me as soon as I walked into the house. It didn't seem like she wanted to ever let go. My sleepin arrangements improved greatly from that first night home, as Mary invited me into her bed.

This time there was no need to whisper. John was not around and not expected anytime soon.

Mary's mouth attacked my mouth in such a way as to awaken every single place on my body. My smolderin passions were excited like never before, if you know what I mean. My arousal was full and complete. I made no attempt to back off. Instead, I fully participated with this excitin woman who opened herself to my every want and desire.

Soldierin and marchin had worn me out. I had rested up in the prison stockade. Now I was bein awakened by the intense lovin. Soon she too had worn me out. She made me lose track of all time for the moment.

I lost myself in Mary's touches and caresses. For a day or two, I completely forgot about the war, my duties to the 2nd Virginia Infantry and everythin else. After all, my Shepherdstown boys didn't know whether I was alive or dead. They were not lookin for me.

What had happened would all have to end soon. I knew that. I also knew I would have to find the boys of Company B and join them wherever they were. But in the meantime, I was not goin to end the bliss any sooner than I had to.

I had been with a few women before, but none like Mary. Since we had shared discussions for many nights, it seemed natural to be naked and lyin next to her.

Not once did either of us mention John and where he might be. I think Mary even forgot about bein married to John. I surely wasn't givin him any thought at all either.

I only stayed for a few days. I needed to catch up with the 2nd Virginia boys. I was told in Shepherdstown that Company B, 2nd Virginia Volunteer Infantry, was camped at Corbin Mansion, Caroline County, Virginia. I said good bye to Mary. I started on my way to find my unit.

I had nearly a week's walk to reach them. On the way I actually did give thought to poor John back in Fort McHenry. I imagined he was quite upset when he woke up and I was gone. I wondered how long he would stay before he signed the oath and returned home.

I gave much more thought to Mary. I wondered what might happen to her and me when the war was over. She was a married woman. That was not helpin matters. I was certainly feelin like we loved each other. It also gave me another person to worry about and hopefully who would worry about me. And someone else to write to.

The boys from Company B were quite surprised to see me. They treated me like a lost son. We traded tales of where we had been since seeing each other.

They talked about a recent battle at Fredericksburg which they called fierce. I was pretty sure it could not have been as fierce as my tales of the battle I had seen in Sharpsburg that they were now callin the battle of Antietam Creek.

I wrote to Mary when I arrived at Camp Winder in Virginia. I told her I missed her terribly and that my heart felt empty for the first time in my life.

What I didn't tell Mary was that my friends from Shepherdstown asked about John. I told them that he refused to take the oath and was at the stockade at Fort McHenry the last time I saw him. I told them he wished me well and told me to say hello to them for him. Actually that was not what really happened. I did not think it was any of their business.

When the earliest days of Spring arrived, the Shepherdstown boys and the rest of our brigade were achin to get back to the war. Winter camp had been long and hard.

The first day of marchin and drillin was through mud holes that had been roads before. My blisters that had healed over the winter came right back as soon as the long days of marchin began.

I got a rather interestin letter at the mail call in April. It was from Mary. She told me that she was having a child and would be deliverin in August. And she added that if she delivered a boy, she would name him Wesley. I was slightly confused, wonderin why she would name him after me. It finally hit me that the child was mine. I was not ready for that information right at this moment, but the longer I pondered the issue, the more I smiled. I was goin to be a daddy.

My first thought had been that Mary and John were having a child. The more I thought about it, the more I realized that couldn't be true. John had not been home. No one knew where John was, except that he was probably still in prison at Fort McHenry. This wasn't John's baby – it was mine. Mary knew that. The idea was just startin to sink into my little brain.

I was both happy and sad. I was happy with the thought of bein a father. I was sad because I didn't think I would be home to Shepherdstown very soon to be with my child and Mary. And I was also sad that the lady now carryin my child was married to someone else.

I wrote to Mary to tell her that her news though surprisin was well received by this little soldier. And that I missed her muchly.

In early May, 1863, word reached our camp that General Stonewall Jackson was wounded in a recent battle. Reports said that he lost an arm but was recoverin from his wounds. He was expected to be back with the Stonewall Brigade within a few months.

Newspapers reported that he had been shot by his own men. General Jackson was a stickler for shootin anyone who did not know the password. In the fog, and without respondin to the call for the password, the sentries had shot him. I prayed for him to recover completely and return to lead our brigade.

Within a few days, the news was worse. General Jackson had contracted pneumonia. He died on May 10. The whole brigade stood silently in morning roll call. Tears fell from many faces as our leader had fallen. A twenty-one gun salute was offered in his honor.

I know some men said they hated General Jackson because he worked us so hard. That was why we were so tough in the battles. But most boys admired and loved him too. For me, it was like I lost a friend though I had never actually met him. I saw him many times leadin the trainin of our boys and commandin us in battle. Love him or hate him – he was a great leader. I was not sure anyone could replace him in the front of the Stonewall Brigade that carried his memory.

His death shook our faith in our brigade. He stood like a stone wall. Stonewalls don't crumble or die. We will fight even harder now, to fight in his name.

As of this day, my shoes had holes in them and my uniform was tattered and torn. I was tired and weary and the hunger tore at my gut. I feared that I had lost so much weight even my own sisters would not recognize me. I was lonely to see them both, but doubted if that would happen very soon.

So far, our company had been shot at, starved, beaten upon by rain, haunted by the ghosts of past battles, baked by the sun, exhausted by the drill sergeants -- yet we marched on. Those federal boys had not gotten the best of us yet. With each fight, we became certain we would win.

Fort McHenry as Civil War Prison
Library of Congress Lithograph – 1861

Fall – Winter – Spring 1862 – 1863
William Esaias Culp

The fall of 1862 wasn't much different than the summer, except like in Pennsylvania, the beautiful color of the leaves was something to see.

While we rarely got to stop and admire them, we certainly were aware of the bright colors as we marched through the forests.

As winter neared, we were still in the western Virginia mountains. Now we were freezing cold. We splashed through icy rivers and streams on our marches. And we still were not finding any rebels to speak of.

In early November, 1862, a fight erupted between two federal regiments stationed here. It resulted in the death of two Union boys – Abraham Fix from Company B and Albert Burner. We were gonna have a hard time explaining to their mothers how they died with no enemy nearby.

In late December, 1862, we marched to Winchester, Virginia. We arrived on Christmas Eve. The town was not friendly to having federal troops around. In fact, one of the Gettysburg boys said he thought the Winchester folks were probably much friendlier to stray dogs than to the federal soldiers.

Our supply wagons had not yet caught up. For Christmas we had salt pork and crackers with our coffee.

In early January, the boys of the 87th Pennsylvania heard for the first time of President Lincoln's Emancipation Proclamation. It was not a surprise as there had been talk about this following the battle at Sharpsburg, Maryland in September. Most of us were not thrilled with the announcement. We had not joined the Union army to fight to free the Negroes.

Gettysburg had a couple hundred coloreds, all free. Several owned businesses. There was a colored shopkeeper, a shoemaker, some laborers and a couple of teamsters. Several of the colored women washed clothes and took in sewing. I knew several and didn't have nothing against them.

I heard the South had four million Negroes in slavery. I wondered where were they all going to go when they were free? How many of them would go to Gettysburg?

Company F got together to talk about what the President said. I think Company F had forgotten what we were fighting for. That was to keep the Union together.

"Are we gonna have colored soldiers now?" John Sheads, Salmone's brother, asked. None of us knew.

"We should vote right now letting the president know that the boys from Company F don't want no colored boys fighting with us," someone in the back shouted.

Everyone was pretty cross with the situation. Jack, who we knew could give a good speech, gave us another – this time about the president's announcement. It calmed the Gettysburg boys down.

I had to admit it. Jack had a future as a preacher after this war is over.

Meanwhile the government in Washington was still behind on our pay. Our Gettysburg boys were ready to go home. The officers had to calm them down to get them all to stay.

The baggage and supplies finally arrived sixteen days after we got to Winchester cause the bad weather had ruined the roads.

I wrote to Annie to let her know that we had been transferred from western Virginia to Winchester, Virginia in the Shenandoah Valley. I told her that we had seen a Gettysburg carriage along the road in a ditch, all broken apart. I recognized the workmanship. Upon a closer look, I was pleased to find my initials marking that I had helped built that carriage.

I told her of Jack Skelly's second speech to the troops, this time asking our boys to be tolerant of having colored soldiers march beside us in battle as President Lincoln had suggested. Annie, I think, will be excited to hear that we were told the paymaster would be delivering our back pay soon.

My letter to Salmone covered the same items I shared with Annie. Of course, I let Salmone know how much I loved her and missed her.

We finally got our pay all squared up in the middle of April. One of the first things I did was send fifty dollars each to Annie and Salmon. I had not much use for the money here and wanted to give it to them to take care of some of their needs back in Gettysburg.

Fall – Winter – Spring 1862 -1863
Jonathan Hastings "Jack" Skelly Jr.

Mother's latest letter found me in Clarksburg, Virginia. I answered back by telling her that all we had done lately was march and drill. I told her that we had split from the main company and were in charge of bringing up the rear with the sick men and all of the baggage. And that although we heard they were close by, we had still not seen any enemy soldiers. Edwin and myself were able to send her thirty-five dollars we had accumulated from various sources along the way.

I told Jennie much the same. I explained that although the area where we marched back and forth was beautiful country, we always had to be on guard that around the next bend was the enemy. After a while, it was almost a joke to mention the possibilities, I told her, because it had been months since we had seen any enemy soldiers. I continued to complain about the paymaster and wondered of his whereabouts.

Meanwhile, I have been sick as a dog. I am recovering from a horrible case of diarrhea. Just now I am feeling much better and am getting stronger. I actually am able to eat and drink for the first time in several weeks.

We marched to Clarksburg, Virginia, the birthplace of that famous rebel General Stonewall Jackson. Someone said we are now 300 miles from home – and no closer to the war than we were at the fairgrounds in York, Pennsylvania. The people here are friendly. They have taken some of our sick boys into their home. Second Lt. Hart is in the hospital. His horse threw him. Our regiment was reviewed today by General Kelly.

We marched to Buckhannon on October 23. We watched the farmers making syrup from the sugar cane. We got to taste the syrup and enjoyed it. General Milroy reviewed our troops. He spoke, telling us that the boys of the 87th Pennsylvania have a good name. He had heard from the citizens here that we are the best behaved regiment to have gone through their town. He told us we should be proud of our reputation and to try hard to keep it. He told us to "let no one sully it but to preserve it above all else." He said we had some hard marching and fighting ahead. With that, he dismissed us.

On November 15 while marching near Beverly, Virginia, one of our men was accidentally shot. The incident occurred in the mountains near Laurel Swamp. Fred Dustman tripped and his gun discharged. The ball went through the knapsack and overcoat of the man in front of him, passing below his ear and out the man's forehead, killing him instantly. The dead man was John Colehouse from Company F.

The men of the regiment were shocked. A group dug a grave and we buried him on the mountain where the incident occurred. An inquiry was held in the death of John Colehouse. It was determined that his death was accidental. I was told that Dustman was changing position of his musket on his shoulder when the hammer of the musket caught on his coat and the musket discharged. Dustman felt terrible. We all did. I wondered who would explain that accident properly for the unfortunate boy's family back home.

I wrote to mother and Jennie. I tried to explain the accident to them as best I could. I told of our continual marches through the mountains of western Virginia in pursuit of the ghosts of the enemy. I complained that wherever we went we were warned the enemy awaited us. And whenever we got there, the enemy had already gone somewhere else. It was virtually a hide and seek operation from beginning to end, with us being the seekers.

In December, I was suffering from a soreness in my breast. When the regiment left, I was unable to go with them. I was left behind with eleven others who the officers did not think were up to marching in the bad weather. Several have been sent to the Grafton Hospital for treatment. I was not among them.

Snowfall and extreme cold were hindering our operations. The snow is drifting making movement difficult. It has been cold enough lately to freeze the horns off of a bull.

Major Buehler left to take command of a draft regiment who would be camping near Gettysburg. He was to report at Washington. I was going to miss his leadership.

Mother had sent gloves for both Edwin and myself. We were grateful.

My letters to mother and Jennie told of my breast pain and respite from marching. I did my usual complaining about the boredom of camp and the lack of presence of any semblance of an enemy soldier. I had read of many amputations in the war and asked a serious question to Jennie. I asked if she would love me any less if I returned home missing an arm or a leg. It was a serious question. I would await her answer.

Colonel Latham had taken command in place of Colonel Hay who was ill. Our orders were to march to Staunton, Virginia along the Staunton Pike with the 12th Virginians with us. Officers told us to be alert due to it being a secesh valley we were entering. Our money would be no good. The valley was fertile, with many animals including cattle and sheep grazing in the fields. We ate chicken, veal, beef, geese, mutton, along with rolls with honey and butter. We grabbed about one hundred fifty head of cattle. Meanwhile our gear did not catch up with us. It rained hard on many days, with our clothing dripping with water.

Our boys marched through Wardensville and then onto Camp Springs where we slept in a building on soft mattresses to stay out of the elements. It was the best night of sleep I had gotten in as long as I could remember. The following morning we marched to Strasburg, to Middletown and then to Winchester.

We were told when we reached Winchester in late December, 1862 that we had marched over 182 miles – from New Creek to Cheat Mountain, to St. George, to New

Interest, to Beverly, to Buckhannon, to Elk Water Fortifications, back to Beverly, to Philippi, to Webster, to Clarksburg, back to Beverly, to Hightown, to Seneca Rock, to North Fork, to Dry Fork, back to Beverly, to Webster, back to New Creek, to Petersburg, to Strasburg, to Middletown, to Newtown, to Kernstown and finally to Winchester. And during that entire period, I never saw one rebel soldier.

The war that I had so anxiously joined had gone somewhere else, leaving the 87th Pennsylvania behind. And I wondered what I was doing to help put down the great southern rebellion that threatened to destroy the Union.

The war continued on. I was not the best soldier. I had never been away from home. I missed Jennie. I missed my mother. I would never admit that to anyone but I was aching to go home.

My favorite part of Mr. Lincoln's Union army was the day my name was called from the mail carrier. Edward Reinecker was our regimental postmaster. I accused him of calling my name last at every mail call to annoy me. He denied that. I was fortunate because several men of Company F had never had even one letter arrive with their name on it. William and I often heard our names called out.

I got comfort in reading and re-reading letters from both my mother and my girl – Jennie.

Tonight I took my shoes off and put my feet in the cool stream near our tent. I tried to think of the last time that my feet did not hurt. I think it was probably back when I was too sick to march. I wished I could soak my feet in this stream for about a day or two. I thought then they might feel pretty good.

All I knew was whatever relief my feet were feeling that night, when we start up the marching again in the morning, the pain would come back.

The boys from Gettysburg were the best of our regiment. We stuck together, and watched each other's backs. The marching and drilling were exhausting. I was wondering how my father was holding up to the difficult routines, as he was so much older than the rest of us.

Major Buehler had left to take command of the conscripts from Cornell. Some of us thought that Major Buehler did us badly for leaving after bringing us out here in the hinterlands of western Virginia.

Samuel George left here today. Edwin and I sent a bundle of clothes home. We got much needed new pants this week. Barney Aughinborough was trying for a discharge and was returning home. He would deliver my letters to Gettysburg.

There was a fight in Moorefield today with our cavalry. Four ambulances from here helped to pick up the pieces of those who didn't walk off the field without help from others.

Shortly we arrived at our new winter camp in Winchester, Virginia. Unfortunately our supply wagons had not caught up with us due to the poor condition of the roads from the snow.

As the new year started, I answered letters from both Jennie and my mother. Mother had said rumors were flying around Gettysburg that all of Company F had been killed. She was grateful that was not true. So was I.

Captain William Martin took Major Buehler's place. He was going to take some getting used to.

Company F held a gathering right after the first of the year to discuss the proclamation President Lincoln made regarding freeing of the slaves. There were questions from the boys from Gettysburg, but very few answers. Some of them were very cross with the president.

I decided to do what I had done before. I decided to take a chance and tell them what I thought. Here's what I told the boys of Company F.

> I spoke to you men before and you all paid attention. Many told me later that what I said made some sense. They appreciated my talk. Tonight I will let you know again where I stand. And like before, you can take what I say or leave it.

President Lincoln took me by surprise by freeing the slaves. But being that we are mostly Pennsylvania boys, we have no slaves. Some of you may know coloreds back home like Abraham Bryan, or the Craig, Fagar, Redding or Little families. We all took a liking to Butler our colored regimental cook, God rest his soul. And you all know the one colored man in our regiment, Greenburt Robinson.

Are coloreds going to be enlisted beside us soon? No one knows for sure. But if we ever get in a battle, do you really care what color the boy is next to you, or are you going to be more worried if he's gonna stand and fight?

In Company F, right here today, we've got boys whose ancestors are Irish, German, English and the like. We're all Americans, Company F, 87th Pennsylvania Infantry, U.S. soldiers. And we are all proud of it.

If President Lincoln, the man who called us to war to help save the Union, says we need to make all slaves free, that's good enough for me.

All of us signed on for the duration of the war. What does freeing the slaves or colored soldiers have to do with our staying the course?

We need to quit complaining. Use your time to write home and let your mother know that you are doing well. Or take the time to work on your musket, in case you ever have to actually shoot at a rebel soldier. Rest up. We are wasting our time debating the subject.

Remember what General Patterson said when we first crossed into the South? I remember. He said "You are not trained to think or make decisions. You are trained to obey orders. Do that and we will be victorious."

Let's leave the thinking and decision making to President Lincoln. As for Company F, return to your tents, get a good night's sleep, and prepare to receive and obey your orders.

I walked away. I went to my tent. William and his cousin, David Myers, joined me. They brought me a fresh cup of coffee. They offered me their thanks. They said I made a lot of sense. And they teased me, calling me "Father Skelly". They asked me to bless them before they went to bed. I threw my coffee on them. That was all the blessing they were getting from me.

I felt proud. Perhaps I did have a calling to the ministry. I would have to think on that matter some more.

Jennie's letter arrived at the end of the month with the answer to the question I had asked previously. She promised that she would not care any less for me if I came home missing an arm or a leg or both. I was happy to hear that.

I wrote letters to her and mother letting them know that I was at winter camp in Winchester, where we were housed in a newly built fort. I told them we had been informed that we would not be marching very far for the next several months. That was good news for all of us. I let them know that the paymaster was expected soon and that I would send them money to help out.

About this time I started hearing from some of the other Gettysburg boys that they were receiving news in their letters about Jennie and what was happening to her in Gettysburg. They talked of her seeing a soldier and staying out late with him. I was angry and puzzled at the same time. Why would my girl be doing that?

I wrote and asked Jennie was happening. While waiting for her answer, I asked Mother to find out what was being said. I told her "The boys here tell me that my girl Jennie has been keeping company late with the soldiers from the 10th New York Cavalry stationed there. Be discreet, please mother, but I desperately need to know." I told her about my speech before the soldiers of the 87th Pennsylvania and that she could be proud of her son. I suggested she might consider that someday I could be a preacher.

Jennie wrote that she denied being out so late but she didn't deny that she had some company. She said she was just being nice to soldiers who were stationed in Gettysburg and that she hoped wherever I was camped, some ladies of the area would take care of me too. She apologized and said she had no idea what she was doing would have been hurtful to me. It was my picture she carried and looked at daily. It was me that she prayed for each day. I was the only one who had her heart's attention.

As far as I was concerned, that cleared up the matter. I promised not to ask again.

Mother wrote in early March to tell me that the Honorable E. McPherson had given my brother, Daniel A. Skelly, a conditional appointment to become a cadet at the U.S. Military Academy at West Point. He was to report between June 1st and 20th. She said she was not quite sure what a conditional appointment was but told me that the letter came directly from the Department of War and said right up front, "you are hereby notified that the President of the United States has this day (dated February 25 of this year) appointed you (Daniel) a Cadet in the service of the United States."

Mother said in a follow-up letter that Daniel "will be duly examined for admission and will be admitted if he is examined and found proficient in his course of study and if his personal, military and moral deportment are favorable."

Everyone in Company F was excited about Daniel's news. He had turned eighteen in December.

When Edwin and I enlisted, Daniel was too young. He accepted instead the responsibility of being there for mother. Edwin and I thought it an exceptionally good idea because Daniel's schooling, at least for a while, would keep him off the fields of battle. And we thought it was also a good place for him to become a man. In fact, I thought it was a much better place for him than where we were.

I wrote to Mother congratulating Daniel and asking some more questions about Jennie.

It had been six months that we had been waiting for the government in Washington to straighten out our pay. When the pay master finally did arrive, instead of killing him (which many of the men had suggested), we held our hands out greedily to grab for the money. We each received seventy eight dollars. It was more money than I ever had in my hands at one time. Edwin and I sent one hundred thirty dollars to mother by Salmone Culp's brother, John Sheads. I sent ten dollars to Jennie to help her and her family.

At the end of April, Edwin was put out of commission temporarily by a bad cold. He refused to go the hospital but was rested when we marched and drilled.

Mother thanked us for the money in a letter in early May. She said Daniel's paperwork for the academy had been completed and that he would be leaving the last day of the month.

The war was suddenly closer than we thought. The 13th Pennsylvania Cavalry got into a scrape with the rebel boys, losing six killed and eight wounded. They had pushed back Imboden's men, who we had heard so much about in our adventures in western Virginia. We missed out on the action again.

On May 3, our regiment and three other regiments of infantry, three regiments of cavalry and six pieces of artillery under command of General Elliott marched 28 miles to Strasburg, Virginia. We arrived there about 4 o'clock in the evening. Our cavalry and the rebels were fighting when we got there. The cavalry drove the rebels from their position into a pine thicket. The rebels took possession of the hill again before we had our dead and wounded off the field. We were ordered to take the hill. We charged. They broke and ran so we could get our dead and wounded. The hill was so steep that we had to crawl on our hands and knees.

One of their prisoners told us that we had given them more trouble than any other regiment that had followed them. It was some of the same crowd that we chased through the mountains last fall.

SIR:

 You are hereby notified that the President of the United States has this day conditionally appointed you a Cadet in the service of the United States.

 On repairing to West Point, in the State of New York, between the *15 and 20 of June* next, and reporting yourself to the Superintendent of the Military Academy, you will be examined for admission into that institution, and if found, on due examination, to possess the qualifications required by the circular hereunto appended, you will be admitted conditionally as a Cadet, to serve until January next, when you will be examined before the Academic Board of the Academy upon the studies pursued by your class prior to that time; and should your proficiency be found to be such as to warrant a reasonable expectation that you will be able to master the remaining portion of the course of study, and should the stated reports as to your personal, military, and moral deportment be favorable, your warrant as Cadet, to be dated *July 1st*, 1863, will be made out and transmitted to you. Should the result of this examination be, on the contrary, unfavorable, your appointment will not be confirmed, and you will cease to be a member of the Academy; but still, in case of good conduct in the several respects noticed above, you will receive an allowance for travelling expenses home, and will be honorably discharged or permitted to resign. Your attention is particularly called, for information on this and other important matters, to the circular hereunto appended.

 You will immediately inform this Department of your acceptance or non-acceptance of this conditional appointment. Should you accept it, and repair to West Point, and report yourself as above indicated, your pay as a Cadet will commence, if you pass your examination for admission, on the 1st of *July* next; but unless you report yourself at West Point within the time specified, your appointment will be recalled.

 Your acceptance must be accompanied by the written consent of your parent or guardian (as the case may be) to your signing articles, by which you will bind yourself to serve the United States eight years, unless sooner discharged; which period will be computed from the time of your admission to the Military Academy.

 It is proper to observe that this appointment confers no right to enter the Military Academy unless your qualifications agree to the letter with the requirements annexed hereto.

Daniel A. Skelly
17 Congt Dist Penna
Care Hon E McPherson
17 Congt Dist Pa

Edwin M Stanton
      Secretary of War.

Daniel Skelly's admission papers to West Point

Fall – Winter -- Spring 1862 – 1863
Mary Virginia Wade

This fall brought a grand harvest of apples. We made applesauce for one week straight, canning about six bushels. The smell of applesauce in the house temporarily replaced the smell of gloom that had been hanging around for quite a while.

I loved the changing color of the fall leaves. On Sunday after church, we traveled the roads of Adams County in a neighbor's buggy to take in the beautiful scenery. It was a rare treat and a chance to forget for just an hour or so the terrible heavy burden the war had brought into our home.

I kept up my letters to Jack on a regular basis. I told him that Georgia and I recently visited Michael Crilly who had been sent home on medical leave to recuperate. I told Jack that Michael seemed quite ill still.

Jack continued to write faithfully to me letting me know what was happening in his world. He told me recently to remind him to tell me after the war how important my letters were to his well-being on a day to day basis.

In the fall, Louis McClellan joined the 165th Draft Militia. He and Georgia had a tearful time as he departed. In fact, Georgia cried for days and days. With his leaving, Georgia and I spent more and more time together. I was especially interested in getting more answers to my questions about her married life.

In December, we were troubled by the news that Louis had been captured and sent to a rebel prison in Suffolk, Virginia. At least we knew that he was in no danger from minie balls or cannon fire.

I wondered how many of the boys Gettysburg sent to battle would return home? How many would be maimed for life? Jack asked me if I would love him any less if he came home missing an arm or leg. Of course, I told him it would make no difference to me. But would it make a difference? I was really not sure. Would his embrace be different if he only had one arm? Could I love him if he had a stump instead of a leg? I really was not certain how I would react. But when he asked in his recent letter, I was quick to point out that I would care no less if he were missing parts of him.

Jack's response became my favorite of all the letters I have received from him. It was the letter I carried in my pocket each day along with his picture. The letter told of his great love for me and his thoughts of me that kept him sane in the insane world of the war. He told me that while other soldiers often received no letters at mail call, he always received at least one letter, usually from me.

With the recent arrival of the Porter Guards around Christmas, boys from the 10th New York Cavalry stationed in town, I was missing Jack slightly less. I wrote to Jack that the Porter Guards were in town and that his friend Jim Hussey asked about Jack. Jim had been captured near Warrenton, Virginia and recently paroled. I let him know that Georgia was very troubled by the news that her husband, Louis, had been captured and was being held in a prison in Suffolk, Virginia.

Mother, Georgia and I often helped by repairing the uniforms of soldiers passing through Gettysburg and providing vittles and fresh water. I have even invited several to church services at St. James Lutheran Church.

Jack had recently written to me from camp in Virginia complaining that I was "keeping company so late". That comment hurt me.

I had thought, being that Jack was hundreds of miles away and concentrating on the war and protecting our country, he wouldn't find out what this girl was doing back in Gettysburg. But someone told him. And it got me into loads of trouble with him.

I wrote Jack several letters angrily in response. Didn't he trust me? I explained that the Porter Guards were nothing to me. I was just being hospitable to some boys who were here, because they too were a long way from home and trying to be good soldiers. I even hoped some young lady in the town with the 87th Pennsylvania unit was treating him and the Gettysburg boys well too.

I tore up those angry letters before I finally wrote one I was able to send. I apologized to him but also told him I had made no attempt to deceive him about anything. I had invited the Porter Guards to church services. I reminded him that I carried his likeness in the pocket of my dress every single day and looked at the handsome soldier many times. I assured him that no other soldier got my thoughts, letters and prayers like he did. I also told him the exciting news that my sister Georgia was expecting a baby sometime in the early summer.

Jack responded to my letter about the Porter Guards and the church incident better than I would have expected. He said "I should have trusted you and not believed the boys here who were getting their information second hand. I have about as much faith in the author of the rumors as a worthless set of dogs. The matter is closed."

I was reminded in the middle of April that the darn war was now starting its third year. Newspaper accounts told of troops starting to move out of their winter camps. They would start fighting again in earnest now that Spring had arrived.

With the arrival of Spring, I started to have more positive thoughts. I loved the new growth and buds on the trees and the blooming of the daffodils and crocus. The blossoming of the fruit trees was always something to be seen around Gettysburg, as there were orchards in every direction.

But along with the optimism of the Spring came the uncertainty of the war. Gettysburg was getting along without our boys and men. The ladies here were mighty unhappy those that they loved were still gone. And their return was uncertain. No one saw any end in sight to the dreadful war.

Part VII

Early June 1863
John Wesley Culp

In June, we were ordered to march again to Winchester, Virginia. We had been there before. I remembered we had not done so well at Kernstown when General Jackson got bad information about the troop strength of the Union boys.

This was the first time the Stonewall Brigade was marchin without General Stonewall Jackson. This time we were goin to give the enemy all they could handle.

And that's exactly what happened. On June 14, our brigade pushed the federals back with a grand rush, yellin at the top of our lungs, and shootin everyone in sight. Durin one portion of the battle, I was pretty sure I was standin face to face, only about thirty yards away, from the boys from Gettysburg. It's hard to know with so many of the enemy blastin away at us, while we were tryin to knock em dead. But they were lookin mighty familiar, if you know what I mean.

Between our muskets and our cannon, we blasted them, showin no mercy. Their lines folded. Soon they were on the run. We chased them clean through town and out the other side. The people of Winchester cheered for us.

Late Sunday night, we were marched toward Charlestown. We were told the federal boys were retreatin in that direction and we were supposed to head them off. They were goin to be real surprised, cause they didn't know we were in the area. Our officers ordered us to keep quiet and rest on the ground with our arms. The federal army was just a few hundred yards off.

We marched quietly to what was called Carter's Woods at Stephenson's Depot just a couple of miles north of Winchester. Our artillery boys set up on the railroad overpass in the pitch dark. Our officers told us the federals would need to cross that bridge to escape. We were goin to block their way.

In the middle of the night, our battery opened fire in the direction of the federal army. The night was so black all we were able to see was the burst of light at the end of each cannon. I don't know how our artillery batteries knew where the enemy was.

Federal muskets fired back at us. But they didn't know where we were either. They were just as blinded by the darkness as we were.

The 2nd Virginia Infantry was held back so we could hit their flank when given the orders to proceed.

When the fightin began, we were awaitin our turn. Just as it was startin to get light from the sunrise, the federals started forward. We waited some more. And then the orders were given for us to charge. We hit their flank hard. They didn't act like they even knew we were around. Their line collapsed. We had them surrounded. Many of their boys ran to save their lives. Others lay wounded on the field. We grabbed about 300 as prisoners.

I asked a couple of soldiers what unit they were with. They said the 87th Pennsylvania. I asked if any Gettysburg boys were with them. They said the Gettysburg boys had been here. And I was bettin some of them that we had captured were boys I might know.

I looked over those soldiers who had surrendered. By golly, there was William Ziegler who I knew from Gettysburg. He told me that my cousin David Culp and a few other Gettysburg boys had been captured. And he told me my old friend, Jack Skelly, was lying wounded somewhere on the field.

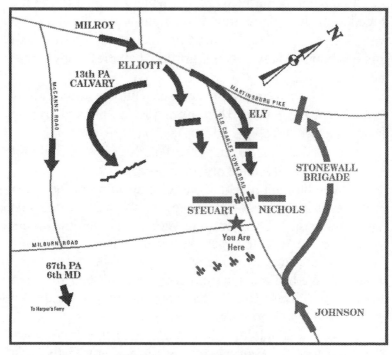

Battle of Second Winchester
Map Courtesy of Virginia Civil War Trails

Early June 1863
William Esaias Culp

As June of 1863 arrived, I wrote to my wife Salmone and my sister Annie to tell them where I was and how I was doing. In my recent letters I told them I was doing well. I complained of the boredom of camp and the constant marching and drilling. We knew the drill in our sleep, but never quite got the chance to use it to help the President save the Union. I often thought that as a federal regiment, we were as useless as teats on a steer.

It seemed that the government went out of its way to keep our regiment out of difficulty. It made me doubt what would happen to our soldiers if we ever encountered an enemy who had already been battle tested. I was not sure we could identify a Confederate soldier if we saw one. The last one we actually had a good look at had been more than a year ago.

In the middle of June, we got in a clash with the enemy at Winchester, Virginia. It was like nothing our boys had ever seen. The fighting was intense, with soldiers falling all around me. I kept my head up and went through the manual of arms as quickly as I could. Line after line of rebel soldiers faced the 87th Pennsylvania lads. Each time we held our ground.

We did lose a boy early in the battle. He was the drummer for the 87th Pennsylvania, 18 year old David Karnes. That death was the first death in battle for our boys.

I am happy to report that I killed my first enemy soldier today. I watched my ball knock him over at about ten yards as his unit came forward into our lines. I hit him square in the chest. It was not pretty. But it was certainly a good shot. I have been practicing on the range for a long time.

I felt nothing for the lad who went down. It could have been anybody. It made no matter to me. I was doing what I needed to do. Shooting him felt good. President Lincoln would have been proud. *That one was for you, Mr. President. I hope to get you some more soon,* I thought. I was hoping there would be many, many more.

We were making the best of the day. With each rebel boy who fell, we gathered more confidence that the day would end with our Union boys the victors.

The cannon fire shook the ground, but never really bothered me, except for the noise. Arms, legs and heads suffered the brunt of the cannon shot. It was the minie balls I feared the most, as I saw many a ball strike one of our boys and put him to the ground in pain.

Among the horrors of the field was hearing the screams of the soldiers on both sides. I could not get that sound out of my head.

As the next line of rebels advanced to within twenty yards, Bernard Cole, one of the Gettysburg boys, yelled, "I get to shoot the littlest rebel soldier," pointing to the spot in the rebel line where a real small boy was marching toward us.

I froze. I would know that little boy anywhere.

"Don't shoot him," I screamed. "That's my little brother." And indeed it was. There marching toward us and to his death, for sure, was Wesley.

I felt sick. He was the enemy. But I could not shoot him, even after all my target practice where I imagined killing him. Even though I thought he was a traitor. Even though I had disliked him every day of my life.

The noise of the battle was so loud I was afraid the Gettysburg boys wouldn't hear me. "Don't shoot the little rebel," I screamed again and again. "He's my brother."

They shot at everyone else – but no bullets were fired at Wesley Culp.

Soon after that, the battle turned sour. Our boys were outnumbered. The retreat was sounded. I skedaddled along with the others. We ran for our lives.

We were beaten badly that day in the field and retreated back to camp. Everyone from Company F seemed to be safe. They joined me. "Your little brother should be dead tonight. Why did you tell us to hold up? He's nothing but another damn rebel," they insisted. And they were right. He looked like any other rebel. He had a gun and was trying to kill us.

That event really troubled me. I couldn't get it out of my mind. Mother and father, who had both already passed, would have called me "a good boy" for protecting Wesley from harm. My commanding officer would have had other ideas. I worried I might be punished for my actions. Perhaps I would be hanged for neglecting my duties. At least a stay in the brig was possible.

I had shot at targets practicing to kill my own brother. And when the opportunity presented itself, I could not watch someone kill him. Was I a coward? It seemed so to me.

After the fight, I walked out to the edge of the camp where I could be alone and fell to the ground. I started to cry. The war had become personal on that day, in Winchester, Virginia. Our divided house brought us to the point that Wesley almost died at the hands of the 87th Pennsylvania – the boys from Gettysburg – his brother, his friends, and his neighbors.

I had saved his life that day. And I didn't think Wesley knew it. I didn't think he had any idea that we could have easily killed him.

There would be other days. Would I be able to shoot him the next time I saw him? I was not sure.

We marched north from Winchester where we were ordered to a position along the Martinsburg Turnpike near Stephenson's Depot at the Winchester and Potomac Railroad. We settled in. We were ordered to stay alert, not build any fires, and talk softly.

In the middle of a very dark night, we heard loud noises and saw flashes of light as artillery shells exploded near us. Orders were whispered down the line to form up. We marched down a narrow road, not being able to see anything until the light of the cannonade flashed across the sky. I stumbled several times in the dark. Others ran into trees and fell in ditches along the pike because they couldn't see where they were marching. Companies in front of us were wheeled into formation. They charged the artillery positions. I was sure that they could not see their hand in front of them either. It seemed crazy for our army to be fighting in the dark.

The fighting continued for a long time. Our company was held back in the woods with many of the others. Trees and limbs fell all around us as the artillery bombardment continued. Several of our boys were hit and went down. I couldn't tell who they were in the dark. Some of our boys were screaming out in pain. But there was no one who could run to their aid.

As the sun finally started rising in the east, we were ordered to wheel about and charge the rebel position. I heard the command loud and clear. "The Eighty-seventh will charge the battery."

Finally in the light we could at least see where they were. But now they could see us too.

We charged ahead. The field was littered with Union boys already. Some were very still. Others were calling for help or trying to get back up.

We passed by them and pushed forward toward the enemy battery on the high ground. Just when I thought we had the upper hand, rebels hit our flank. I don't think our officers knew they were coming. The whole right flank of Company F collapsed and disappeared. I lost contact with many of our boys. One minute they were there beside me. The next minute they were gone.

Finally, the order was sounded for us to fall back. Several of our company ran back to the safety of the woods, while others kept on running. As we retreated, the rebel guns fell silent for the first time.

This was the day, after all the days of marching and drilling, and searching for the elusive rebel troops that we had prepared for. We had trained for this for over two years. We had finally gotten our chance. And we had not done well at all.

Perhaps we were not prepared for a fight in total darkness. Perhaps there were too many rebels at this place. Or perhaps the rebel soldiers were better fighters than we were.

Whatever the reason, we would have to lick our wounds this day and bounce back hoping that on another day we would do better.

The 87th Pennsylvania moved on, retreating toward Charlestown and Harpers Ferry. The Sheads boys, David Myers and I were given permission to wait throughout the day for our boys who were missing in case they returned to the battle scene. We were told to catch up when the others arrived. By this time it was pretty much every man for himself.

Missing from Company F were Jack and Edwin Skelly, my cousin David Culp, Billie Ziegler, Billie Holtzworth, Jacob Rice, and H. H. H. Welch. They were part of almost three hundred from our brigade who were missing and not accounted for out of just less than a thousand who had reported for duty.

The following morning we checked again. They were all still missing. We waited another whole day with no results. All of us were greatly disappointed that we did not find our friends. We decided instead of joining our boys in Charlestown, we would take a much needed and very unofficial furlough in Gettysburg. But we had to be careful, because officially that made us deserters too. We headed out with no information on our friends.

General Robert Milroy
Union Commander at Second Winchester

Early June 1863
Johnston Hastings "Jack" Skelly Jr.

In early June I took time out to write to let mother and Jennie know my whereabouts and situation. I told them of our encampment in Winchester, Virginia.

Winchester was in the Shenandoah Valley. The area was rich in supplies needed by the rebel army. Our orders this time and every time were to keep the enemy from their supplies. I read that Confederate General Stonewall Jackson had said that "If the Valley is lost, Virginia is lost." It seemed like a good time for us to try to see to it that we took the Valley from them.

Some days that meant tearing up their rail lines. Some days that meant setting up lines of defense south of town facing up the valley, in case the enemy came a calling. Either way, on most days, we preferred a fight of some sort to just marching and drilling.

We had been in service for over two years and had only been close to one battle. That was on our first day in the South. We had not seen the enemy since that day in very early July 1861.

In the middle of June, we got ourselves into a fight. I got off some good shots at the rebel boys and hit one square in the face. He fell forward and did not move. I felt sick. Even in a battle, I really wasn't keen on killing anyone, even if they were the enemy.

We faced Wesley's regiment today. I saw him marching toward us. His brother, William, screamed for us not to shoot him. I do not know what got into William. But God bless him for what he did today to save Wesley's life. Sad to say, the rebels got the best of us. Many boys lives were lost on both sides. We got pushed hard and retreated.

That same evening, General Robert Milroy ordered our men to retreat toward Charlestown. Us boys of the 87th Pennsylvania formed up under General W. L. Elliott's Second Brigade. We were commanded by Lt. Colonel John Schall. We marched near Carter's Woods which is north of Winchester and near Stephenson's Depot. We were ordered to have our arms loaded and to be ready for action.

I never expected that the action would begin during the night. The rebel army must have known where we were cause they started pounding our position with artillery fire. We formed up and marched in the dark.

Marching in the dark against an enemy I could not see scared me. I flinched every time I saw the flash of their cannon.

Limbs of trees crashed down upon us as we marched. Men tripped over each other trying to stay out of the way of the artillery canisters. As we marched, the rebel artillery battery continued to shell us. They were directly in position to be between where we were and where we needed to go. Our officers sent companies ahead of our line into action to take out the rebel battery.

After several hours of fighting, the artillery was still hammering us. When the first rays of sunlit lit the field, Company F and others were ordered to wheel into the battle. Our orders were to attack the battery to protect our line of march. I was on the right flank with Company F and most of my friends from Gettysburg.

When the fight began, we fought gallantly. But we did not make much progress. As we charged ahead, a rebel unit surprised us by hitting our flank. We were unguarded on the flank. Our line crumbled. We were surrounded.

I looked around. Several of the Gettysburg men including myself, William T. Ziegler, Billie Holtzworth, Jacob Rice, David Culp, H. H. H. Welch and my brother Edwin were ordered to surrender.

We had talked often about this very situation. If we got captured, we intended to act like we were surrendering. We were to count silently to five. When one of our boys yelled "five" we were all supposed to run like hell. We had laughed about the plan. We thought the rebels would be so surprised that we would have a few minutes to get away before they recovered from their shock.

One of our boys yelled "five." I started running as fast as I could. For about ten strides I thought the idea was a good one and that we were getting away. But some lucky rebel boy fired into our boys. I took a hit in my right shoulder. The ball knocked me down. I tried to get back up, but I couldn't move. Blood was spurting from my shoulder. Billie Ziegler stopped to help.

I laid face down on the ground in intense pain. I had never felt pain like that in my life. When I looked up, everyone I saw standing around me had gray uniforms on except for Billie. The rebels boys told us we were their prisoners.

At that moment, I was not sure whether the other Gettysburg boys got away or not. We had been told that if we ever got captured, we would be exchanged for rebel prisoners within a short time.

I had never planned to become a prisoner of war. I had never planned on being wounded. Now I was both. I wondered if today, June 15, 1863, would be my last day on earth.

The rebels took Billie with them and promised to send back some medical help. I was not trusting that a rebel soldier would keep his word.

As I lay there, I started thinking about the rebel soldier I had shot. Had he laid on the field and thought about home and his family and loved ones. Or had he just fallen dead.

I thought about mother and Jennie mostly. The pain increased as the time went by. Mother. When I gave you my ambrotype and said "If I fall in battle, you will know how I looked before this war brought sorrow upon our land." I had no idea that I had done it just in case this very thing happened to me.

I thought of my wonderful Jennie. Was this the end of me? Would she now marry someone else? I couldn't stand that thought.

And for the first time I actually thought about all the men, dressed in blue and gray, who had fallen, like me. I wondered if they had gotten a chance to think about their life like I was doing now. I was thinking about who I had become and whether I had made a difference on this earth.

I started to pray with more fervor than I ever had, asking the good Lord to have mercy on me. I asked that I be given a chance to live and to return home, if that was His will. I was thinking along the lines that in returning home, perhaps I could be a better husband and father than I had been a soldier. And that perhaps I might become a minister and spread His word. Even with that, I knew it wasn't my decision.

I finally decided that all I really could pray for was a chance to get a message to mother and Jennie. After that, God could take me if He decided that was best for everyone. And that was my prayer.

I don't know how long I lay on the field. It seemed like a long time. The blood continued to flow. The pain did not go away like I was hoping it would. I thought I might not make it off this field.

Early June 1863
Mary Virginia Wade

I prayed and prayed that the boys of Gettysburg would be spared and sent home. I was impatient, even though I knew they would return in God's time, not Mary Virginia Wade's time. Even so, it was not comforting on any level. In fact, it was down right unsettling to my soul.

With every single passing day, I was getting more annoyed at my friend, Jack, who had not written me recently. His last letter was dated June 1. That was not like him at all. He had been regular as clockwork. All the women in Gettysburg were keenly aware that my stack of letters from Jack was higher than any stack in town. And many were jealous about that.

I had recently talked to Jack's mother. She had not heard hide nor hair from him either. I felt sorry for her having two boys who had been away from home now for a long time. Fortunately her husband had recently returned home from the war. Her son, Daniel, had recently left to attend the U.S. Military Academy at West Point.

Georgia's belly was getting larger and larger as she got closer to delivering her baby who was due at the end of this month. Her clothes had to be altered to fit. She often was too sick to help me with our chores.

I remained optimistic, refusing to think the worst. I imagined Jack to be quite busy marching and drilling and probably quite exhausted from all that going on every single day. I didn't want to think that he might possibly be sick.

Besides, it was hot and dry outside. I was not sure he was getting regular amounts of food. He was probably thirsty. And he surely wasn't comfortable or getting a good night's sleep in a tent.

Still, he owed me two letters now. And deep down inside I was taking it personally. I was hurt.

Mother and Georgia tried to console me. Georgia had only had a few letters to read cause her Louis rarely wrote to her. Even Georgia was a little put out that I didn't get a recent letter from Jack.

Life in Gettysburg had not changed much at all. About the only thing anyone had to look forward to were the newspaper reports and the letters from the boys.

Rumors had been flying around town for the past several weeks that there were rebel troops close by. Each time the ladies of the town became upset. And each time the rumors were exaggerated to the point that it seemed more likely that there were no rebels at all anywhere close.

My family was getting tired of the false information. But we weren't stupid. We were on guard for anything.

We leaned on each other for strength. The older men left in town promised to be vigilant and keep us posted. The business men actually had a plan. If the rebels came this way, they were going to hide their merchandise so that the rebel soldiers couldn't get a hold of it. They didn't want to have their merchandise stolen or paid for with the worthless currency of the Confederacy. Some even planned to ship their supplies by rail to Philadelphia if necessary.

A committee had been formed to develop a plan to defend Gettysburg if that were ever needed. They were to report back at a town meeting.

Pennsylvania Governor Andrew Curtin let us know that he had our best interest in mind and would be the first line of warning if anything were happening that we needed to worry about. He also promised that the federal army would protect us if needed.

I knew that General Robert E. Lee had brought his soldiers into Maryland in September of 1862. The federal boys held them off in Sharpsburg, Maryland. The rebel boys had their stay cut short. Since then the war had been quite far away. And that suited the people of Gettysburg just fine.

Part VIII

Late June 1863
John Wesley Culp

I was determined to search for my friend Jack after the battle at Stephenson's Depot. I would search until I found him. That's cause he was my best friend. I didn't care how long it took. The war could wait. I wasn't goin to let him die alone on the field.

After about two hours of searchin, I did find Jack. He had a terrible wound in his shoulder. I tore my shirt and bandaged it as best I could. The bandage turned red from the blood, but at least the bleedin stopped.

He told me that my brother had seen me on the field several days before and told the Gettysburg boys not to shoot at me. I could not imagine what got into William. I thought he would want to shoot me himself.

I waved to get the medics to come help. They helped me lift Jack onto the gurney. I helped carry him into town to the Taylor Tavern that was servin as the hospital. Our medics promised to help him as a favor for me.

Jack begged me to come back the next day and take messages to Jennie and his mother. I promised him I would. But I told him it was not real likely that I would be in Gettysburg soon. He knew that. I was hopin he actually would get well and go home before I had a chance to deliver the notes.

The following morning I returned to the hospital to visit Jack. He gave me two sealed notes, one addressed to his mother and the other to Jennie Wade. I promised faithfully to deliver them personally whenever I could. We shook hands and wished each other God Speed. I left knowin that he was in good hands at the hospital.

Shoulder injuries left soldiers with a handicap. He might not be able to use his arm again. Doctors might even cut his arm off. That was certainly possible. But Jack without an arm was still better than most boys I knew who had all their parts. His injury might get him a medical release so he could go home to Gettysburg and not have to fight again. I did not think his wound was mortal.

Following our victory at Winchester at Carter's Woods, Company B of the 2nd Virginia was ordered to march north – not knowin exactly where we were goin to end up. But I did know we were near Shepherdstown cause I was recognizin the territory. Before we bedded down Major General Edward Johnson spoke to us.

Men. Soon we will be crossing the Potomac River with our whole army of almost 70,000 soldiers. When we cross the river, we will be in the North. We will be in Maryland where you can expect some fine welcoming and some annoyance – cause the people of Maryland haven't quite decided which side of the war they want to be on. Be nice to these folks. Perhaps we can convince them to favor us. Pay for any vittles you take. Be polite. Be grateful.

General Lee himself has passed the word down the line – all men in his army are to treat civilians humanely. He does not believe that wanton destruction of property in our enemy's lands will advance our cause. We will not make war on defenseless citizens, women or children.

Save your ammunition for those damn Yankees we may be running into soon.

This is probably the most important campaign of the entire war. Success here will lead to a complete Confederate victory and the end to this dreadful war. We will succeed. I am confident that your training and drilling have prepared you for what lies ahead. Rely on that training and your drill to get you through the day.

March with your heads held high as proud soldiers of the Confederacy. President Davis knows you are preparing for this invasion and wishes you God Speed. We will move out tomorrow at first light. Men, be prepared to march to your destiny.

Our boys were excited. We had no idea we were part of such a huge army of men.

Henry Kyd Douglas stopped by camp and found me to say hello. He had been an aide to General Stonewall Jackson and was now an aide to Major General Johnson. Douglas was goin to march with us. He reminded me of the night we had burned the bridge here early in the war.

Douglas said the Stonewall Brigade would be part of the larger army of General Ewell. He told us the whole rebel army including General Robert E. Lee was many miles behind us. We were to meet up with other divisions that would cross the river near Williamsport.

On June 18, we broke camp and began our march. I was excited about goin near Shepherdstown. I hoped at least for a glimpse of Mary. In the early morning we marched down the road lined with people from town like a parade in the early morning. The whole town seemed to be cheerin and clappin and just enjoyin seein the former Hamtramck Guards returnin home. I was sure that many of the boys had not been back since the day we were all mustered in back in 1861. Their families were lookin for them in our lines.

I was not disappointed. I saw my dearest Mary waving a hanky, lookin very much full with a baby inside her, and runnin toward our Hamtramck men, lookin for me.

The whole line halted. Mary finally found me and hugged me heartily. "My dearest, Wesley. You are lookin weary, but are a wondrous sight for my eyes to see. Return soon my dear." She kissed me and pulled my hand to her belly to feel the baby growin within.

Some of the local people called out my name. I gave them a little salute. It was nice to see them again.

My eyes teared as we continued our march to Blackford's Ford. Many of the locals followed us until we reached the ford.

I was certainly familiar with Blackford's Ford – havin crossed with John in September of 1862 to help General Lee at Sharpsburg. I alerted the men on either side of me to be aware that the river water was much higher on me than on them. I didn't want to be washed downstream. The water was cold and refreshin but not deep at all like it had been when we had crossed before. The water was the bath I had not had in months. And even though the water filled my shoes and was not soothin very long, it comforted my achin feet and the blisters from all the marchin.

After crossin the river, we marched through the old dry canal bed. Our army had broken the canal so that the federals would have trouble takin supplies down the canal to the capital in Washington City. That had been our mission at Hancock the previous winter – to breech the dam so that there would be no water gettin into the canal.

After we crossed the river and canal, I looked behind. The line of our army was as far as I could see. There were many thousands now crossin with us into Maryland.

Some locals walked amongst us, welcomin us into Maryland. Several waved our beloved stars and bars flag at us. They gave us food and drink. They said they would pray for our success. Others looked at us from their yards or porches, not lookin like they'd be prayin for our success at all.

We marched into Sharpsburg. We passed the battered little church where John and I had been captured and stopped to set up camp on the very fields where we had fought so mightily. The place was real quiet. There were no minie balls or cannon balls flyin here and there. No dead and dyin soldiers were lyin in the fields. But there were mounds of dirt I was certain were graves of men who had fallen here.

If I had not been here before, I would not have known that a great battle had taken place here. I told those boys with me tonight that this was where the famous battle of Antietam Creek had taken place. I told them what I knew about that battle. None of our Hamtramck Guards exceptin John and myself had been to the battle that was now known as Antietam Creek.

Several men found ripe cherries near by and brought them back for us to munch on. I had not had anythin so delicious in many months.

The Shepherdstown boys teased me rememberin that was John's wife who had kissed me a few hours before. They said they were puzzled that she kissed me. They told me they remembered me sayin that John refused to sign the oath and was in prison – wonderin how his wife was now with child. I wasn't about to tell them the real story. And they were not about to let me off the hook for some information.

I made up a story about Mary writin me a letter tellin me that John had died and that she had remarried – tryin to get them to believe that she only came lookin for me cause I had lived in their house. I was not sure they believed me – but the teasin let up.

Actually I was real proud to soon be a papa – though I was troubled that Mary certainly wasn't my wife – and in fact, was someone else's wife. I didn't think they needed to know all that at this time. I didn't like lyin much. I was brought up better than that. I didn't even want to think of which of God's commandments I had broken makin a baby with John's wife. But then I remembered that God didn't approve of no killin either. That was a commandment too. But He certainly had given us this war to fight. I was hopin God was on the rebel side of the war.

The followin mornin we broke camp and marched north on the pike toward the town of Hagerstown, Maryland. The rain continued to pelt down upon us and muddy the roads where we marched.

The general had been right about our welcome in Maryland. Some houses were boarded up with no one in sight, probably afraid of us rebels and what we might do. Others brought their babies in their arms, their children holdin on tightly and waved to us, offerin water and bread.

We stopped often in our march so those behind us could keep up. Once we were held up for some time due to a dispute. Seems a toll taker would not allow the army to pass by without someone payin the toll for each man. Imagine an invadin army havin to pay toll to go to war in Maryland.

The dispute was finally resolved when Henry Kyd Douglas, who was known by the toll taker, gave him a note and promised to have old Jefferson Davis pay the tolls.

In the afternoon, the rain stopped as we marched through the streets of Hagerstown. There we found the quiet cheers and the wavin to us at some places, and empty streets and boarded buildins at other places. The children pointed me out as I marched by. One even begged his mother to let him join up too.

We camped north of town. Officers let us know that by early mornin we would be in Pennsylvania. My heart and thoughts turned to my family in nearby Pennsylvania. I was closer to them that I had been since the war started. I wondered about my two sisters, Annie and Julia. I thought about mother and how I missed her. And I wondered where my brother William was on this very day.

I thought too about Jack Skelley. Was he goin to make it back home? Our hospital in Winchester was certainly goin to treat him as good as any place. And I thought about my friends and my cousin, all from Pennsylvania, now bein held in a Confederate prison somewhere. Would they be exchanged and be able to go home soon too?

I overheard men talkin about the awesome army we were part of. It was said General Lee's army extended all the way back from here to Culpeper, Virginia. I could not imagine that many men. I was mighty glad they were with us. I was determined to make General Lee proud. I was certain we could beat the Yankees and end this dreadful war.

On the mornin of June 20 around ten in the morning, we crossed into Pennsylvania. One of our bands stood at the state line playin "Dixie". I was back home. Well, not quite. I was probably within marchin distance from my home in Gettysburg. We were told here to try to pay for anythin we took with Confederate dollars. The rule was if the folks wouldn't take the money, we were to take what we needed and give them a receipt so they could claim their loss.

I was troubled by bein in my home state. I had joined the army to protect our homeland. I had not joined to make an attack on my old home state of Pennsylvania.

There seemed to be some mighty hard feelins with the ladies of Pennsylvania in particular. They didn't like it none that we were stealin bread, chickens, hams, and most anythin else we could find. Several of the women were so angry they were heard swearin just like a man. I didn't blame them much. But since the Yanks had stolen chickens, hams and nearly everythin else in Virginia, it served them right to be gettin some lessons about what happened in a war here in the North.

Our long lines of rebel soldiers trudged onward, marchin northward to Greencastle. When our boys marched through the town, we were an impressive sight, with over 200 cannon, plus ambulances and supply wagons stretchin in a line many miles long.

We camped just north of Greencastle. Some of us were sent to Marion to destroy the train bridge there. We pulled up miles of rail and ties. We burned them in fires. When the rails got hot, we bent them around trees so when they cooled off, the rails could not be used again. We took the bridge down with axes and explosives. We also captured some Negroes. We had been told to round up Negroes as they had fled the South. We were goin to return them to their proper owners.

Today General Ewell's carriage passed along side us. General Ewell had lost a leg in the war, but continued to lead his boys. He could no longer ride his horse.

We marched to Chambersburg on the followin mornin. We were surprised that the road here had been paved by some hard material. It was somethin I had never seen before. It was tough on my hurtin feet too.

When we arrived, our band played "Bonnie Blue Flag" as we marched through the square. We camped north of town. Throughout the whole day, we didn't hear one word of encouragement or anyone cheerin us bein in the North. We got no offerins of food and water. After all, we were the enemy. They did not even care that I was a Pennsylvania lad. They saw my gray uniform and they hated me along with all the boys on either side of me.

Our soldiers were sent in all directions to steal vittles for our men from the locals. We stole horses and wagons as we continued marchin. We marched north, through Shippensburg and Newville and then to Carlisle.

We were told that we would be campin for a few days in Carlisle. We set up our tents at a college called Dickenson. The 2nd Virginia boys rested and waited. Several men took shots at the metal mermaid up atop the main building until the officers scolded them for wastin good bullets we should be savin for the Yanks.

Men listened as I told them about bein from Pennsylvania. They thought it quite laughable that this rebel soldier had grown up on Yankee ground. But they also admired that I chose to be a rebel, where they generally became a rebel cause they were born in the South. Somehow that made me feel real important.

At Carlisle we were mostly glad we were restin instead of marchin. Marchin gets real borin. It made me tired all over. Sittin on the ground in Carlisle was nice and restful. It was easy duty. But we were told to be ready at any minute, because a major battle was a comin our way soon.

Knowin the lay of the land around here, I was pretty sure we were headin to make some trouble at the nearby state capital in Harrisburg. That was right up the road from Carlisle. I was hopin we were not goin to get orders to burn the capital city.

We were all invited to attend the Lutheran Church services in Carlisle on June 28. I was talked into goin by some of my friends. As it turned out, it was actually upliftin for me to spend some time in prayer with the others. The preacher read a Bible passage from one of the Psalms sayin "depart from me, therefore, ye bloody men." I'm thinkin he said that on purpose cause we were there. It was funny too because it was said that General Ewell was asked to pray for the President. The General refused. He did, however, add, "I am sure he needs it."

For some reason we had all been spared by the Almighty up to this time. I'm thinkin the good Lord must have had somethin to do with it – it could not have been all luck.

On June 29, we broke camp in Carlisle. Instead of marchin toward Harrisburg, I saw some local landmarks I recognized and believed that we were marchin close to Gettysburg. I was shocked to hear that we were marchin toward home. Officers told us they thought that was where the battle would take place.

Gettysburg, I did not think, could have a major battle the likes of which I had seen at Antietam Creek and Bull Run. I feared my home town would not survive all the death and destruction. I did not like the idea of fightin in Gettysburg. But I was only one lad – and no one from either side asked me if I thought Gettysburg was a good place to fight.

It did appeal to me that I might get to see my sisters, while there. And, of course, a chance to deliver Jack Skelley's messages to his mother and Jennie.

As we marched, I could not help but think of home. I thought of Annie and Julia. I thought how they were more than likely scared to death with soldiers marchin into the town. I hoped everyone I knew was safely hidden away.

Memories of growin up in Gettysburg took over my brain as I marched along with the others. I thought of all the adventures that my friend, Jack Skelly, and I shared. And I wondered if our rebel medics were treatin him well at the hospital in Winchester. I even wondered about William and the boys from Gettysburg. I thought of the ones we captured in that last battle, and fretted about how long they would have to stay in the stockade before their exchange came through. William, I was certain, escaped. I had no idea where he and the others might be.

Our regimental bugler woke us up early the followin day. We marched through some more familiar ground toward where I called home. It was the 1st day of July.

Before long, we could hear the cannon and musket fire. The noise got louder as we got closer. I could feel the cannons shakin the ground as we got within range. Smoke filled the air, along with the all too familiar smell of death.

Major General Edward
"Old Alleghany" Johnson

General Richard S. Ewell

Late June 1863
William Esaias Culp

I finally found out officially that all except one of our men who had been missing had been captured at Carter's Woods near Winchester. Jack Skelly was not on the prisoner list. He was officially listed as missing in action. The prisoners of war I was not worried about cause I expected them to be exchanged. I feared the worst for Jack.

I walked to Harpers Ferry, crossing the river and continued to Frederick, Maryland. I took time out to write letters to Salmone and Annie about our recent disaster at Winchester. I listed the local men missing and presumed captured, including men they would know – my cousin David Culp, Billie Holtzworth, William T. Ziegler, Edwin Skelly, Jacob Rice, and H. H. H. Welch. I told them there was no accounting for Jack Skelly, except that he was officially listed as missing in action. I said I was not sure where I would be going, not wanting them to know that I was walking toward home.

Several of the Gettysburg lads had decided to walk back home with me. We were tired and beaten. The battle in many ways had been a disaster for the 87th Pennsylvania. So many of our men had been captured.

We had been routed by those damn rebel lads. That was bad enough. What was even worse for me personally was that I failed when I had a chance to shoot my brother, the traitor.

All those troubling thoughts had made my walk back to Gettysburg quite depressing. I only wanted to rest up a bit before catching up with Company F again.

I reached my sister Annie's house on Friday, June 19th about 10 a.m. Annie and Julia took me in. They sent a message to my wife, Salmone, to join me there. When she finally arrived, the three women doted on me like I was a king returning to his castle. I liked the attention. They asked about the others. My letters to them had not yet arrived. I didn't tell them about the prisoners or about Jack Skelly because I didn't want to alarm them.

I debated whether to walk to see Mrs. Skelly or Jennie Wade to tell them about Jack. I didn't think it would help them to know. In fact, I thought they would be frantic. So I didn't tell them anything.

I was pampered with fine food. I was able to sleep in a real bed with Salmone. I also got the news that General Robert E. Lee's army had marched into Pennsylvania. It seemed like they had followed me home. I didn't like them coming here at all. I wanted to shout out, "Leave us alone. Go back to the South where you belong."

I feared for my neighbors and for my little town. I had seen what the war had done to Winchester, Virginia. I did not want that to happen here.

But if they were coming, I was determined to stay home and protect my wife, Salmone, and my sisters, Annie and Julia. They had no one else but me. I was in the position that my brother Wesley had offered for joining the rebel army. I was going to protect my homeland from the invading army.

Reports were passed around town almost hourly, letting us know that parts of the huge rebel army were now in Carlisle and Chambersburg. Since Carlisle was to the north, I was thinking that maybe they were going to Harrisburg, the capital of Pennsylvania.

But almost as soon as I got those thoughts in my head, someone brought the news to Annie's house that the federal army was marching through Emmitsburg, within ten miles directly to our south. It was said that they were coming to Gettysburg.

Late June 1863
Johnston Hastings "Jack" Skelly Jr.

As I lay wounded and perhaps dying on the field of battle from my shoulder wound, the familiar face of my old friend, Wesley Culp, appeared in front of me. At first I thought I had died and was in heaven. But he spoke. "Jack, are you all right? Can I get you some medical help?"

"Wesley, you rascal. What are you doing here?" I asked, while at the same time watching Wesley tear his shirt and provide a bandage to my bleeding shoulder.

"I saw my ugly brother's face over yonder hill. I almost nailed him with a minie ball between the eyes," he told me. "At the last second we both recognized each other and hesitated. If I had that to do over again, I would still like to shoot him."

"He's a better shot – always has been. It would have been you who would have been the goner," I insisted. "He actually called off our firing when he saw it was you. I swear to that. I was there."

"You asked why I am here. After the fightin was over, I thought I might check on the prisoners to see if there was anyone out here I might know. I found Billie Hotlzworth and several other prisoners includin my cousin, David Culp. Holtzworth said you were lyin on the field wounded and might need help. He gave me some idea of where you had fallen. I looked around until I found you."

The medics arrived. Wesley helped them put me on the stretcher and carry me to the hospital. "You're gonna be alright, I reckon," he assured me. "We've got good medical people with us. I'll tell them to take good care of you, even if you are a bloody Yankee."

"I'm not going to make it, Wesley. The medic said I lost too much blood before you came along. Can I count on you to take messages back to Jennie and my mother?"

"You'll be fine, Jack. But to humor you, I will agree to take the messages back to Gettysburg. I hope you aren't in a hurry about the delivery. I haven't been back home in six years or so."

"Promise me, Wesley, that you'll do it. And then I can die in peace," I begged.

"I promise, Jack. But you ain't gonna die, my friend. Boys who get hit in the head, the chest, and in the gut die from their wounds. You have a shoulder wound that should heal over time. In fact, I'm thinkin you'll get back home before I will. And it's not goin to be in a pine box."

"Come back later. I will have the notes for you. And thanks, Wesley."

Wesley did return again the next morning. I handed him two sealed notes. One was addressed to my mother. The other was addressed to Jennie.

"God speed, my friend. And thank you for helping me off the field and having them bring me to the hospital. I'd have surely been dead already without your help."

"Take care, Jack. You'll be on your feet soon. But keep your head down."

I was at peace. God had given me the chance to write letters back to my mother and Jennie. That is all I asked for. Now my life was in His hands.

Calling the place where they were taking care of me a hospital was comical. It had always been called Taylor Tavern prior to the war, I was told.

The medics didn't have to look very far to find whiskey to use for medicinal purposes. The nurses, in fact, snuck several swigs to me daily for the extreme pain in my shoulder.

Convalescing in Winchester gave me a lot of time to reflect on this awful war. Like everyone else, I was surprised the war was still going on.

I had gotten the news here that many from our brigade, perhaps as many as three hundred, were now rebel captives from the fight where I was wounded. They were probably being sent to prison camps in Richmond, Virginia. That did not seem all bad, because I was certain they would be exchanged before too much delay.

I had also been told the rebel army was now massed and heading into the North. That was troubling to me. I had read previously when Robert E. Lee had resigned his commission with the U.S. Army prior to the secession of Virginia, he had done it to protect his homeland from the invasion of the North. I would not think attacking the North was part of that idea at all.

But in some ways it made sense to me. We had destroyed General Lee's supplies and food as we marched through the Shenandoah Valley. He probably thought it was time to bring some destruction into the North in retaliation.

It was troubling for me to figure out what winning a battle or the war would bring to the victor. Each side was losing so many boys. Even when a battle was won, it seemed to me that the cost was too high. When would the madness end?

Here at the hospital, boys lay in every direction from me, hurting terribly from this awful madness called war. They were all rebel boys except me.

Meanwhile, my wounds were not healing. My shoulder still hurt like hell. The pain I thought would eventually lessen had not. The surgeon told me I was real lucky to still be alive. He said the infection in my shoulder was more his concern than the wound itself.

The nurses continued to comfort me and encourage me. One said that I was certain to be home in Gettysburg by September. I was thinking that I might make that trip in a pine box.

I continued to pray. I knew that I was in the Lord's hands, and that no matter what I did, His plan would prevail. I was comforted by that. My worries were minimal. Perhaps God was pleased to think I might be a preacher after the war.

I thought of Wesley and how he searched for me on the field where I fell and how he brought me here. Only a good friend would have done that. I was grateful. His promise to take my messages to mother and Jennie was also a comfort to me. Wesley always kept his word.

I found it remarkable that with so many battles across this huge country, our Gettysburg boys had been up against Wesley's Virginia boys twice; once at Falling Waters and now in Winchester. The odds of that happening had to be astronomical.

Each time I closed my eyes, I knew there was a possibility I would not wake up again. But I was not fearful. I was much safer in Taylor Hospital than I would be marching with the 87th Pennsylvania, wherever they were today. I trusted the medics and nurses here. Even though they were southern sympathizers, they were taking care of me as if I were one of their boys. I found that remarkable too.

I had fought for a worthy cause. I was proud to be a soldier in the army that President Lincoln called to save the Union. I was pretty sure, in spite of recent setbacks, eventually the federals would win. The country would be saved. I though it too great of a country to dissolve and fall apart.

If I had it to do over with, I would still have enlisted and fought with the Union. I may, however, have surrendered when the rebels surrounded us, rather than trying to run away. That was how I got shot.

My thoughts often were about marrying that pretty young Jennie. I could not even think of who she might marry if I didn't get back home alive. I remembered asking her in a letter if she would love me if I were missing an arm or leg. She said that she would not love me less. I was counting on that.

I worried about my brother, Edwin, who was both wounded and captured. I had not received any news of Edwin.

The nurses brought me writing paper. They thought I might like to write home. I was too weak to write. And I had already given Wesley my notes to the women I loved.

I knew my mother and Jennie would be worried that my letters had stopped.

Our regimental surgeon, William Francis McCurdy, who had been captured along with the others from the 87th Pennsylvania, was assigned duty at the Taylor Hospital. It was great to see someone I knew. He was assigned to my case and took good care of me.

Several times religious men came by to comfort me. We prayed together for my healing. The rebel ministers seemed sincere, even though I was clad in blue.

David Eberhart, the regimental chaplain for the 87th Pennsylvania, was a frequent visitor too. He told me of the devastating loss the regiment had suffered in the battle. He said we had eleven killed, twenty one wounded, and two hundred seventy three captured.

The food at the hospital was not bad. Often I was not very hungry. Their soups were most welcomed. I hardly missed the hardtack and awful coffee that we lived on as we marched.

The nurses open the windows because the heat was stifling. That way at least there was a breeze drifting in at times. I was fairly comfortable most days if you don't count the pain in my shoulder. I slept peacefully whenever I was tired. I felt like I was resting in the palm of God's hand.

Taylor's Tavern used as a Confederate hospital
Winchester, Virginia
From the James E. Taylor's Sketchbook
The Western Reserve Historical Society
Cleveland, Ohio

Late June 1863
Mary Virginia Wade

In the last days of June, 1863, I was worried for Jack's safety. I have complained to my family and his that I have not received a letter for more than three weeks. That was not like Jack at all. His letters were regular as a clock.

But I had other worries during those days.

For about the tenth time in the last few months, reports were floating around Gettysburg that the rebel army and General Lee were coming our way.

I heard news in town that William Culp and several of the Gettysburg boys had returned home. I wanted to run over and talk to William to see if he had any news about Jack. I was too busy to fret about Jack for the moment due to all the duties I was responsible for.

Those of us left in town met at the courthouse. Several of the older men gave speeches. They insisted that we all hide out in our cellars and stay out of sight. But they had no answer as to what to do if the rebels started setting fire to our homes. If that happened, we would all die and be permanently sealed in the cellars of our homes.

Mrs. Skelly and Annie Myers, William Culp's sister, spoke up. They said we had an obligation to help the Union soldiers when they arrived. Yes, they thought we should be safe and protect our families, but when the going got tough, we must help our Union boys.

The other women of the town cheered in support. Georgia and I were determined to help, however we could. But we would also do anything in our power to keep our families and our valuables safe at all times.

My little brother, John James, was now seventeen. He finally wore mother, Georgia and I down, begging us to allow him to enlist. He joined the Adams County Cavalry commanded by Captain Robert Bell on June 23. I was deeply troubled by his enlistment, but agreed to alter his blue uniform so at least he looked like a soldier. He was to be the regimental bugler.

I continued to faithfully write to Jack, even though I was not getting any response. At least that helped me deny that anything bad might have happened to him.

In my latest letter to Jack I told him I was worried because he hadn't written. Perhaps, I said, he was too busy to write. I told him of my little brother joining the cavalry. I begged him to write and give me comfort in knowing that he was alright.

On June 26, the rebel soldiers were said to be approaching the town of Gettysburg from the Chambersburg Pike. We feared what their arrival in town would bring. Governor Curtin and the local newspaper had both issued warnings to the residents and business owners of the borough of Gettysburg to be ready to protect themselves and their belongings.

I worried about my sister, Georgia, and her new baby, Louis Kenneth, born on that same day – the 26th. I helped with the delivery and watched the tiny child being born. It seemed like a miracle to me.

In these troubled times, I tried to comfort Georgia as she tried to comfort me.

I saw Daniel Skelly in town on June 28. Jack's mother had told me that Daniel had an appointment at the United States Military Academy at West Point and had started there on June 3. As soon as our eyes met, Daniel dropped his head. I asked him why he was already home.

"I ain't supposed to tell no one," he said, with his eyes still avoiding mine. "You won't tell no one will you?" I promised, though I didn't know what could be so bad that he couldn't look me in the eye to tell me.

"I've been rejected by the academy....based on my academic record," Daniel said almost soft enough that I might not have heard if I hadn't been paying really close attention. With that, he ran down the street, not looking back.

His mother and father must be devastated, I thought. *Two boys in the war and now another son rejected by the official Military Academy of the United States.*

I was sure that Jack would be furious if he knew about the situation with Daniel being discharged from the academy. Perhaps his mother had already told him.

I fussed with the baby, Louis, to take my mind off my worries. He was so little. I held him like he was mine, wondering what it would be like to be a mother. Georgia seemed so well prepared to take care of a youngan. I was not so sure how I would be as a new mother. Georgia had a real hard time delivering her baby and was bedridden.

I preferred my boys to be a little bigger and to be able to take care of themselves. I wondered if Jack Skelly would make a good father. I would not want my babies to grow up having a father like the one I had been given. I said a silent prayer that God would bless my troubled father wherever he may be.

In preparation for any upcoming troubles, we moved to my sister's house on Baltimore Street where we thought we would be safer. After I made two trips carrying six year old Isaac Brinkerhoff, the boy who boarded in our house, and my eight year old brother, Henry, I locked the house and went to stay with the rest of my family.

As the rebel army approached town from the north, we heard reports that the federal army was approaching from the south. I thought that strange. It seemed like they were all coming from the wrong direction. And destined to clash right here in Gettysburg.

When the Union army finally arrived, the women of the borough, including my mother and myself, were busy baking bread for them. Many soldiers knocked on our door and needed water. I filled my bucket hundreds of times for the federal boys.

I worried about my twelve year old brother, Samuel, who had been captured by rebel soldiers just a few days ago. He has been released because my mother approached General Early. She told him Samuel was just a boy who was running an errand. The general kept the horse Samuel had been riding, but released my brother. For now we have Samuel hidden safely at Mr. Pierce's house.

Mother complained every time I went outside. "It's not safe out there, Mary Virginia," she shouted. "Didn't you hear that Governor Curtin told us to stay inside?"

"Mother. All my life you have taught me to reach out and help others in need. These men are thirsty. It's hot. They need cool water. I am just trying to help," I screamed back.

"Keep down when the bullets start flying," mother requested.

I laughed and told her, "There isn't a soldier from either side who is going to shoot a girl."

As the rebels approached and the guns started firing, General Early's men knocked on the doors of the people who lived in the area and begged us to stay in our houses for our own protection. I, for one, would never have disobeyed that order. At least if we stayed in the house we would be safe.

The only ones left in Gettysburg were the women and children. Most of the men were gone to war. Only the elder ones were still here. I am thinking that most of our boys are in Virginia, trying to bring the southerners to submission.

Now the entire rebel army was about to attack us – the innocent people of Pennsylvania. We had done nothing to them. We should not have been a target.

I was scared and angry. But I was also determined to not go down without a fight.

Part IX

July 1, 1863
John Wesley Culp

Company B of the 2nd Virginia Infantry was assigned to Major General Johnson's division. We arrived in town in the afternoon and were ordered to guard trains arriving in Gettysburg. The town was quiet. Word was that for that day our boys had been successful. I was dismissed from duty around 3 o'clock.

I stopped by my company commander's tent to offer my assistance. "Private John Wesley Culp, Company B, 2nd Virginia, Stonewall Brigade, sir," I announced, snapping one of my best salutes as I entered his tent.

He returned my salute. "At ease soldier. How can I help you?"

"I thought I might be able to help you, sir. I grew up in Gettysburg. I know much of the land. As a youngster, I explored this whole area. I can tell you what I know to see if it might be of use to our army."

"I think that information might be useful. I will send a messenger to command headquarters to see if they want to talk to you. Wait here, sir," he said.

I felt good. Finally I might actually be helpful. Most days I didn't feel of much use to the Confederate Army. Oh, sure, I was shootin and marchin like the rest. But I wasn't bein of any more use than anyone else. Today I felt like I might be able to give our officers somethin that could help our rebel boys win this battle.

Wasn't too much later I was shown to a small stone house along the Chambersburg Pike. The officer announced me as I followed him through the doorway. "Private John Wesley Culp, Stonewall Brigade" was all he said. I saluted and was brought forward. I recognized General Robert E. Lee, our commanding officer. There was several other generals present. My old friend Henry Kyd Douglas was in the back. He nodded to me. I am not sure who the others were.

"We understand, soldier, that you may have valuable first-hand information concerning the land here," General Lee commented.

"Yes, sir. I grew up in Gettysburg. I would like to be as helpful as I can, sir."

They asked me to step forward and discuss with them the terrain around Gettysburg on a large map they had spread out on the table. I spent probably two hours pointin out the area around the town as I knew it.

After helpin them, I sought out Captain Benjamin Pendleton to see if I could get a pass to visit my family. Captain Pendleton had known me from Shepherdstown.

Captain Pendleton said as the captain he could not authorize a pass for me. But he did offer to go to General James A. Walker and ask him. He told me to wait for him. In about ten minutes he was back, sayin that General Walker would like to see me in person in his tent. Captain Pendleton led the way.

At General Walker's headquarters, we waited no more than a few minutes before we were shown in. Captain Pendleton introduced me. I saluted. General Walker returned the salute. And then he shook my hand. He said, "I am pleased to have a Pennsylvanian in my brigade. I heard that you already have helped our officers with your knowledge of the area, which I appreciate," the general said. "Certainly I will issue you a pass for this evening to dine with your family. Be sure to be back in camp tonight as we have much work to do in the morning."

I thanked General Walker and Captain Pendleton. I assured them that I would return later tonight.

It had been over six years since I had been home for my mother's funeral. I thought about those years as I walked the two miles from camp to my sister's house.

My thoughts turned to wonderin about William, my friends and neighbors, who were all fightin for the enemy now. I thought for the first time of my decision to move to Shepherdstown with the carriage business. And I realized how that had led me to put on the gray uniform of the rebel army.

There was no turnin back now. I had made my decision. I was happy with my choice. I was a true southerner now. Our cause was a good one. The rebel army was growin stronger and beatin the federal troops at many of the battles along the way. I was amazed how large our army was.

The closer I got, the more familiar the houses became. I tried to remember which family lived in which house. And I wondered if the town of Gettysburg could withstand a major battle here.

I arrived at my sister Annie's house on West Middle Street. Her house was right across from Jack and Edwin Skelly's home.

It was not that I had forgotten my promise to deliver the messages to Jennie and Jack's mother. Who would have thought when I promised to deliver them for him I would be participatin in a battle near my home within just a few weeks? My original idear had been that I would deliver those messages when I was on leave or after the war.

It was my intention to take the messages to them after tomorrow's fightin. I think they will be pleased to receive the notes, although I was sure by now they knew Jack was badly injured in battle.

I knocked on the door. A lady opened the door. I did not know her. I told her I was lookin for my sister, Annie. She told me Annie had moved to another house on Middle Street. She pointed down the street to the house. I thanked her and walked to the other house.

I knocked on the door. My sisters certainly were not expectin me. I wondered if they would recognize me. I had

196

lost weight. My uniform was tattered and dirty. I had not shaved or bathed recently.

Annie opened the door, hesitatin for just an instant. And then she rushed out to greet me with a hug. "Wesley. Welcome home."

"Annie. It's nice to be home," I answered. I stumbled up the step and into her house.

Julia ran toward me and put her arms tightly around me. Tears ran down her face. "I'm glad you are home. Please have supper with us. But be forewarned, brother. Some of our relatives, includin William, have threatened to shoot you on the spot if they find you here."

"Doesn't surprise me none," I said with a smile, but at the same time knowin that they weren't jokin at all.

Annie introduced me to her new husband. I had not known about him before. We shook hands. Salmone was seated at the table. When she saw me she got up and left the room.

A few minutes later Salmone returned. Behind her stood my brother, William. I was real surprised to see him. He looked as haggard as I did. His uniform could have been plucked from a rag pile. He gave no idea that he saw me. I nodded to my brother. He turned and left the room. It was like he didn't want to admit I was there. Salmone actually nodded my way but did not smile.

They had just started supper. I sat down and joined them.

I ate like there was no tomorrow. Every time a plate of food passed my way, the plate was lighter as I passed it on. Annie asked me to stay the night. I told her that my pass expired soon. I must return to my company tonight. And then I explained my other mission.

"Coming up through Winchester, I ran across Billie Holtzworth who was a prisoner in our hands," I told them. "He told me about Jack Skelly being wounded and left layin on the field. I hunted for poor Jack. When I found him, I took him to the hospital. I left him in charge of the rebel surgeons. He was shot through the shoulder. He gave me a message which I am to give to his mother. It is late now. I will not disturb her. Please tell Mrs. Skelly I will be back tomorrow evenin. Have her here. I want to talk to her. I'll be back soon."

"No message from Jack to anybody else in Gettysburg, Wesley?" asked Annie.

"Never mind," I said, tryin to get out the door. "You'll get all the news from Mrs. Skelly."

"We can deliver the message for you," Annie told me.

"No," I insisted. "I promised Jack I would deliver it in person. Good night. Thank you, Annie, for a wonderful supper."

"You ought to stay with us all night, Wes," Annie called out as I turned to leave. "We may never see you again."

As I walked back to camp I was not sure why I had not told my sister that I also had a message for Jennie. It was too late to return and mend the error. It didn't much matter. By tomorrow evenin both Mrs. Skelly and Jennie would have Jack's messages in their hands. And I will have kept my promise to Jack to deliver the two messages in person.

When I returned to camp, I told Captain Pendleton of my visit. I told him I was pleased to be able to spend time with his two sisters, but was troubled that my brother acted like I wasn't even there.

"He still dislikes me, Ben," I insisted.

"It has been a rough war for him too, Wesley. Look how we routed them a few weeks ago in Winchester," Captain Pendleton told me.

"He never liked me," I said. "He thinks I am a traitor. Nothing I do would change his mind."

We stayed up most of the night as we often did before battles. Captain Pendleton wanted to know if I had any regrets joinin the rebel army instead of comin home to serve with my brother, my best friend, and my neighbors.

"None, sir," I said quickly. And I meant it. "I think I have served Virginia well. I made my decision and have never looked back."

"And I am proud to have served beside you. You are such a good friend and a good soldier," he said, saluting me as he finished.

I was pleased that the Confederate command had allowed me to provide information that might be useful durin the battles. I was thinkin that with all the hills and ridges in the town, General Lee would certainly pick the best ground for the fight. I was sure tomorrow would be a better day General Lee's army.

Even when the others finally bedded down, at least to try to sleep, I stayed awake. I thought of my mother. I was as close to her as I had been at her services in late 1856. She was restin peacefully at the Evergreen Cemetery near the same ground I had walked tonight. Tears filled my eyes as I thought of how much I have always loved her. And how much I missed her. Tomorrow, after the battles and after delivering Jack's messages, I was determined to find mother's grave and sit a while with her. Yes, I was thinkin, that would be good for me to do.

I was happy to have been able to visit with Annie and Julia tonight. And even though our time was short, I was grateful for the chance to see my sisters. I had never expected to return to Gettysburg only to be preparin to make battle on the same land that I had played on for so many years as a youngan.

General Lee's Headquarters
Gettysburg, Pennsylvania

July 1, 1863
William Esaias Culp

My two sisters and I watched through the closed drapes as soldiers marched by the house. I urged my sisters to stay inside. I was going to stay here too.

Most of the neighbors had either fled town or were going to stay in the cellar for however long they needed to. Fear was the word of the day. Most of the men were already in the war, so the women were in charge. And they were taking no chances at all. They moved their children and their food and worldly possessions into the dark corners of their cellars. They were prepared to stay as long as it took.

Many of the storekeepers had moved their supplies to other buildings for safe keeping. They were certain that the rebels would look to steal whatever they could get their hands on. It was not comforting at all to think that they might pay in Confederate dollars like they had done in Chambersburg. We knew that their paper money was totally worthless.

We heard the fighting start, with the awful noise of cannons and muskets. There was no break throughout the entire day. I had no idea how close the battle was or how many were involved. But it sounded like the whole world was ending on this very day right here in Gettysburg, Pennsylvania.

Around mid-afternoon, Daniel Skelly came by and asked us to provide clothing for bandages and buckets to carry water where needed. He said the churches and the courthouse were filling up with the wounded. He was trying to get some help from every family. Julia begged to go to the courthouse to help with the wounded.

I protested, not wanting her to be in any danger. But Annie and Salmone said someone from the family should help. They thought as long as Julia was with Daniel, she would be safe.

I wasn't sure, but Salmone and Annie had me outnumbered. Daniel pledged to be responsible for her. We gathered all the clean cloth that we had and put them in a sack. I got two buckets from the cellar for them to take. Julia ran off before we changed our minds.

The rest of us stayed in the cellar most of the day. The horrible sounds of the battle never ceased for even a minute until everything got real quiet in the late afternoon. The horrors of war that frightened my sister and my wife nearly to death, shook Annie's house. Even when I closed my eyes, I could see what the battle looked like. I had been through it before. I could see in my mind lads from both sides being blown away in the fighting. But I didn't dare tell them.

Julia returned in the late afternoon. She was a mess. Her dress was torn and spotted with dirt and blood. She was nearly hysterical in telling us what she had seen.

"It was awful," she cried. "Boys were laying everywhere – on the courthouse benches and on the floor. Blood was streaming out onto the floor. Some were screaming. Some were real quiet. Medics rushed from boy to boy to try to help them. Many seemed way beyond help. I tried to pitch in, but didn't know what to do. I got blood on my dress. I got sick watching the doctor saw off a lad's mangled arm. I ran home without even saying goodbye to Daniel cause I was so upset."

She was nearly out of breath and crying between sentences, but continued on. "There are wounded everywhere. Even at St. James Church and at the Catholic Church. The pews are almost full. We don't have enough cloths for bandages or enough buckets to bring water to them. It was dreadful." She fell on the floor and sobbed.

Salmone and Annie pulled her up, trying to comfort her. Suddenly the war had become to them as real as it had been for me. I feared Julia would be haunted forever by the things she saw today. I wish now that I had insisted that she not go with Daniel.

It was not supposed to be like this. The federals planned to go into the South and do their fighting there. Our generals planned to bring them to submission on their own ground. It was to teach them a lesson for leaving the Union.

No one ever thought, even after the short campaign into Maryland when the rebels were stopped cold, that they would return into the North to bring havoc to our quiet little villages.

Wesley had said he was fighting for the South to protect his home against the aggressive invasion from the North. Now I was determined to protect my home from the invasion of his rebel army.

It seemed like the whole world was crashing down upon me and my family.

That evening while we were sitting at supper, I was quite surprised to hear a knock on the door. Not many people were out and about. I stayed hidden in the cellar but listened to see who was calling. Annie answered. Several minutes passed before Salmone came down the stairs to let me know the visitor was my brother. I followed her back upstairs and looked toward him.

I pretended not to see him. I was not at all happy that he was here. In fact, if I had my musket handy, I would have finished the job I had failed to complete in Winchester. I wanted to shoot him dead right there in Annie's house.

Instead, I gritted my teeth and tried to remain calm and disinterested. I turned away and walked back down the stairs. I did not let him know that I even knew he was present. My dislike for him overcame me. Wesley was a traitor. He was dead to me and this family. On another day I would have insulted him and belittled him for his decision to betray us and fight for the enemy. That night I was not big enough to do that.

Salmone told me later that Wesley ate like he had not eaten in weeks. Perhaps he hadn't. I had heard that the federals were doing a good job cutting off the supplies to the rebel army. I smiled inside for being a part of that. I hoped after he left, that he would take food back to the other rebel lads and that they would choke on it.

When he finally left, it was none too soon. My sister Annie ran down the stairs and started in on me after he had left. "William Esaias Culp. You should be ashamed of yourself. You acted like a fool pretending to not know your own brother."

"Listen to me, Annie. Most any other man in Gettysburg would have shot a rebel soldier in his house and earned praise from his family for protecting them from the enemy," I said, more calmly than I would have thought was possible. "I didn't even know that lad who was here except to know that he was a traitor and a disgrace to this family. And it took every ounce of restraint I had not to find my musket and shoot him right here in your house."

Annie started to cry. I let her. This time I knew I was right.

I went to bed quietly. Salmone tried to comfort me, but I was not in any mood to be comforted. I did not sleep. The battle that had started today would be continuing in the morning. I was pretty certain of that. I was not going to participate. If either army searched the cellar and found me, I would be in big trouble.

I don't pray often, but tonight I prayed for the safety of my family. I prayed for our little town. I prayed for my friends and neighbors. And I even prayed for my little brother, Wesley.

July 1, 1863
Johnston Hastings "Jack" Skelly Jr.

I had been determined to take one day at a time here at the Taylor Tavern Hospital. This day was the sixteenth day of my hospital stay. I was being treated quite well by the medical staff here even though their patients were all rebel boys except for a few of us Union boys.

Since arriving I watched as several have passed into the great beyond. A few others were given medical orders to return home to try to recuperate. Even a few had walked out of here to rejoin their regiments.

Going back to Gettysburg to convalesce now seemed a worthy alternative to continuing to stay in Winchester. The doctor said he would give me a medical release when I was strong enough to travel. The thought of leaving lifted my spirits. It gave me even more incentive to get better.

Some days were good days and others were bad ones. Today was not one of my better days. I feared even when I was up and walking around, my shoulder and arm would never be of any use to me. The surgeons had lively debates within range of my hearing on whether I would survive an amputation. Truthfully if it would save my life, they could take my arm and shoulder. I would be willing to go home in that condition.

I had bounced back several times before from bad days. I didn't know why I couldn't bounce back again tomorrow. My nurses continued to encourage me even when the surgeons were less optimistic.

Some days the medical staff ignored boys within days before they died. So far they had not chosen to ignore me. I felt that was a good sign.

The mood here for the most part was dreary. Some of the patients were much more cheery than others. I was certain that had to do with the availability of the hospital's alcohol since we were housed in one of the town's largest taverns.

My cot was located near the main bar. The nurses delivered sips to me when the pain was too much to handle.

All the medical persons here were remarkable. It seemed they were here no matter what time of day or night. They didn't ever sleep. I didn't know what kept them going. They were doing a great service in keeping us alive. Many boys would survive this hospital because of their diligence and dedication.

There have been no new wounded soldiers brought in recently. To me that meant the war had moved somewhere else.

All of my recent prayers were to have God's will be done. I thought of Wesley Culp. I was very grateful that he brought me here and prolonged my life. I thought of my beloved Jennie. My love for her grows. The nurses had brought paper and pencil for me to write to Jennie and my mother. I was too weak to write even a short letter. I worried because I had heard nothing about my brother, Edwin.

My nights were mostly sleepless causing me to be very tired during the day. In the day I had been so tired I had even fallen asleep on occasion in the middle of talking to visitors. I slept in short spells many times throughout the day. My dreams were not comforting at all. My pain did not subside even when they gave me opium.

One of my nurses had told me the last couple of times I awakened from my sleep screaming. I lay sweating on my cot. They said the sweating meant my fever had broken. They said the screaming meant I was vigorously fighting the infection. I fear they were not telling me the truth.

My conversation seemed odd to me. When I thought I was talking to someone my mouth moved but words didn't come out. I didn't seem to be very coherent.

The cot was not as comfortable today. When I moved even the slightest amount, the pain in my shoulder reminded me to be still. Yet to move even an inch assured me that I was still alive.

I needed to hang on, but I was so very, very tired. I tried to sit up. I saluted my nurse and screamed, "Corporal Johnston Hastings Skelly Jr., Company F, 87th Pennsylvania Volunteer Infantry, Second Division, United States Army, reporting for duty, sir."

July 1, 1863
Mary Virginia Wade

I was determined to give any help that I could. Georgia was still bedridden from giving birth and was not of any help to us. She was only able to take care of the baby so Mom and I didn't have to worry about those duties.

I frantically baked what seemed like an endless number of loaves of bread. As soon as I pulled a half dozen loaves from the oven, I put in the same number to be baked.

I filled all the water buckets from our well and filled any containers we could find. The soldiers would be needing water, as the days had been mighty hot.

By late morning, we heard cannons firing, shaking the ground. The noise, even through the walls of the house, was deafening. Mother screamed more than once for me to stay inside. But I couldn't pull water staying inside.

Late in the afternoon we got a message that bandages were needed to help the wounded now laying in the pews of our beloved St. James Lutheran Church and on the benches and floors of the courthouse. I gathered as many rags as were clean and got them ready. A neighbor stopped and offered to take them to the church.

By this time mother was helping me too. We did not speak. We just plowed ahead with the work that we thought would help the cause to save the Union. It was all we could do.

When the fighting ended for the day, a strange quiet was in the air. Every so often a boy would scream out in the dark. We wished we could find him and help him. But there were too many. We could only help those who could come to the house.

Even in the dark, men found us. Some drank water from the metal dipper we provided. Others cupped their hands and we poured water for them to lap up. They took a loaf of bread, often sharing it with another boy behind them in line. And over and over again, they thanked us.

Mother and I were completely exhausted by the end of the day. But we needed to get the yeast ready for morning. There would be more boys needing our help. We would do what we could do. And we were proud to help our boys and our country.

Part X

July 2, 1863
John Wesley Culp

As reported by Captain Benjamin Pendleton, 2nd Virginia

We were called to form up at an early hour on July 2. Wesley Culp and I fell in with our friends of the 2nd Virginia. He and I marched off to battle side by side.

As we approached the Christian Benner farm near Rock Creek, we moved forward from the skirmish lines. For some unknown reason, Wesley peered up over a boulder for a better look. I yelled at him to get down and then grabbed to pull him down. He fell into my arms, dead. A ball had hit him squarely in the forehead during the instance that he looked up. He died instantly.

We buried him in a shallow grave near a crooked tree so we could come back and find him later.

July 2, 1863
William Esaias Culp

All day the house shook as the fighting got fierce. I sat at the top of the cellar stairs, blocking it with my body so that Salmone, Annie and Julia could not pass me. I was not going to let anything happen to them.

They spent the day taking turns praying out loud. When they were not reciting a prayer or Bible passage, one or the other of them was crying.

I was torn between my duty to guard them and my pledge to help President Lincoln's federal army. I wondered how just one more soldier might help. I decided my place was protecting my family.

July 2, 1863
Johnston Hastings "Jack" Skelly Jr.

Jack was unable at this time to correspond on his own. He was lying in Taylor Tavern Hospital in Winchester, Virginia suffering from a shot of a minie ball in his right shoulder.

The following report was filed by John Warner who visited him at the hospital in Winchester, Virginia.

I am a suttler from the 87th Pennsylvania Volunteer Infantry. I have known Jack Skelly from earlier in the army camps. I saw Jack in early July in Taylor Tavern Hospital in Winchester, Virginia. Skelly was delirious. He did not recognize me. Not being trained in the medical field, it is my honest fear that Skelly's wounds are mortal. I don't think Skelly will last long.

The second time I saw him, he did not seem to be suffering. He was just lying in a stupor. The boys in the company and I knew he wrote letters regularly to Jennie Wade of Gettysburg. I was told that Wes Culp carried a message to Jennie from Jack telling that he had been wounded.

July 2, 1863
Mary Virginia Wade

All day long, mother and I baked bread and drew water for the boys. Today was hotter than yesterday. I was sure they were suffering not only from the heat but from their woolen uniforms.

I thought of Jack and how I wanted badly to believe some southern lass was giving him food and drink right now too. I told mother that we had a duty to perform and as long as God kept sending boys my way, it was my duty to serve them. I reminded her of the Bible passage "Whatever ye shall do to the least of my brothers, this ye shall do unto me."

All the boys were tired, hungry and thirsty. Word must have been getting out that our house was helping anyone who came by, cause I had a line of men waiting for me to help them every time I looked up. All were polite and grateful.

I was hoping every soldier who came into the yard was going to be Jack Skelly saying that he was now home. I said a silent prayer and then went back to the tasks at hand.

I told mother that we must start more yeast tonight so that it would be ready by morning. I would be baking some more loaves of bread for the federal soldiers. It was the least we could do for the boys who were fighting not far from our house.

July 3, 1863
Mary Virginia Wade

From official reports

Mary Virginia "Jennie" Wade, died on the morning of July 3, 1863 from a gun shot through the door of her house. Jennie was killed while baking bread in the kitchen of the McClellan House, where her sister, Georgia lived. A stray bullet from a rebel musket came through the door around 8:30 in the morning, hitting Jennie in the back of her left shoulder blade. The minie ball passed directly through her heart. She died instantly.

Jennie Wade was the only civilian fatality of the battle of Gettysburg. Jennie was 20 years old when she died. In her pocket was found an ambrotype of Jack Skelly and one of his most recent letters.

Ironically, Jennie died without knowing that Wesley Culp had died the day before, or that he had a message for her from Jack Skelly, as it was never delivered.

July 5, 1863
John Wesley Culp

As reported by Captain Benjamin Pendleton, 2nd Virginia.

After the battles finally ended, I went to Wesley's sister home to give them the news. Annie's cries drew Wesley's other sister, Julia, who I had met in Shepherdstown, into the room. At the news, Julia cried hysterically. I stayed until they calmed down. I gave them the landmarks so they could find his grave.

Annie and Julia and several uncles and cousins searched for the body. They wanted to find Wesley, dig up his body, and bring him back to the Evergreen Cemetery to be buried alongside his parents.

But the mark was gone. They couldn't find his grave. Annie did find the stock of his musket with "W. Culp" carved in it. The stock of the long barreled gun had been cut down because Wesley's arm was so short.

The messages for Mrs. Skelly and Jennie were lost and never delivered. Ironically, Wesley Culp was the only 2nd Virginia Infantry soldier killed in action at the battle of Gettysburg.

Name carved in stock of Wesley's gun

July 5, 1863
William Esaias Culp

Late in the day there was a loud knock on the door. I feared answering it. So I ignored it. The knocking continued. I heard someone yell that he needed to talk to Annie.

Not wanting anyone to know I was there for fear I would be considered a deserter, I let Annie go to the door. But I cautioned her to find out who was calling before she opened the door, and to quickly close the door when her business was finished. Meanwhile, I got my musket, loaded it and cocked the hammer, just in case I needed it.

Annie asked who was calling. I could not hear the answer but trusted that she knew if she should open the door. The door opened and someone came in. Within minutes, Annie was sobbing loudly, saying "Oh God – No, this can't be true." She yelled for Julia to come up from the cellar amidst her sobs.

Julia pushed past me and within a few seconds, she too was crying out of control. Salmone crept near me as we tried to listen in.

Finally Annie came back down to the cellar and told us that Wesley had been killed. And that they were going out to search for his body. Salmone and I told them to go ahead. They left.

I was stunned. I could not get my mouth to work as Salmone asked me what I wanted to do. All the years I had spent disliking my brother had numbed me to this minute. I did not feel anything. I was neither happy nor sad. I had wanted to kill him myself. Some federal soldier had done my job for me. I didn't know if I was disappointed in not getting the job done myself or glad that he had been killed.

Dammit, Wesley, I thought. *If you had come home and joined with the Gettysburg boys in the federal army, this would not have happened. But no – you had to do it your way. And now look what happened. Is this how you wanted to die, as our enemy? You chose to defend your homeland against the northern aggressors. And your boys end up attacking us and causing us to defend our homeland from you.*

My sisters returned. They had found Wesley's musket but not his body. They told me they had searched where the rebel soldiers had buried him but their mark had strangely disappeared. They were distraught beyond words. I was not in any way able to comfort them.

July 11, 1863
Johnston "Jack" Skelly Jr.

The following report was filed by John Warner who visited him at the hospital in Winchester, Virginia.

I visited Jack Skelly again at Taylor Tavern Hospital on July 11, 1863. Skelly did not respond when I tried to talk to him. Jack Skelly died in the hospital on July 12, 1863.

Jack died without knowing that Wesley Culp had been killed at Gettysburg, that Jennie Wade had been killed or that his messages never got to his mother or to Jennie.

Epilogue

Popular legend suggests Wesley Culp was killed on July 3 at Culp's Hill on property owned by his father's first cousin, Henry Culp. Information taken mostly from Benjamin Pendleton's account (and he was there) indicates that Wesley actually died on the morning of July 2 at the Christian Benner farm near Rock Creek or near Brinkerhoff Ridge. In spite of that fact, the legend always seems to be the more popular alternative.

Jack Skelly was buried in the Lutheran Cemetery in Winchester, Virginia. In November, 1864, Jack's brother, Daniel, returned to Winchester to retrieve Jack's body. It was re-interred at the Evergreen Cemetery in Gettysburg where he now rests only a short distance from Jennie Wade's grave. The Grand Army of the Republic (G.A.R.), a Civil War veteran's group, founded the Corporal Skelly Post No. 9 G.A. R. in his honor.

William Culp saw no action at the battle of Gettysburg. He was promoted to Sergeant Major, March 1, 1864. He was promoted to 1st Lt. Company C on December 13, 1864. He survived the war and was mustered out of the 87th Pennsylvania on June 29, 1865. William considered his brother, Wesley, a traitor for fighting for the Confederacy. William reportedly never spoke of his brother again. William died on October 12, 1882.

Jack's brother, Edwin Skelly, spent time at Libby Prison in Richmond, Virginia following his capture at Winchester on the day his brother was shot. He was discharged on October 13, 1864. He died in 1913.

Wesley Culp's friend, Mary, who had been noticeably pregnant in the streets of Shepherdstown in the fall of 1863, was seen later that year looking very thin. No one ever saw her baby. Persons who lived in her house after Mary left the area insisted that they heard a baby screaming, but never could find the source of the noise. Legend has it that Mary murdered the baby in the basement of that house. That story has never been confirmed. Mary's husband, John, was not ever heard from after she told him to "rot in prison" at Fort McHenry.

Wesley and William Culp's cousin, David Culp of Gettysburg, also of Company F of the 87th Pennsylvania Volunteer Infantry, was captured at Carter's Woods in the battle of Second Winchester, on the same day Jack Skelly was shot. He was sent to Belle Isle Prison in Richmond. On July 14, 1863 he was exchanged at City Point, Virginia and sent to Camp Parole near Annapolis, Maryland.

Jerry Sheffler of Gettysburg, who moved to Shepherdstown with Wesley Culp to work at the Hoffman Carriage company and also enlisted in the 2nd Virginia Volunteer Infantry. He lost an arm in battle, probably at Cedar Mountain. Sheffler moved to Toms Brook, Virginia and raised a family. He died in 1913.

Henry Kyd Douglas, aide to General Stonewall Jackson and then aid to Major General Johnson after Stonewall Jackson's death, was wounded and captured at Gettysburg. He was taken to Jackson Island Prison in Lake Erie and then transferred to the prison at Point Lookout, Maryland. He was exchanged on March 17, 1864. He survived the war. He died on December 18, 1903.

Members of both the Skelly and Wade families, depending on the source, either confirm or deny the story of a possible pending marriage of Jennie Wade and Jack Skelly.

The Characters

John Wesley Culp
Born 1839
Petersburg, Pennsylvania
Died July 2, 1863
Gettysburg, Pennsylvania

William Esaias Culp
Born August 8, 1831
Died October 12, 1882 in Petersburg, Pennsylvania
Married Salome Sheads 1853

William Culp grave

Salmone Culp grave

Johnston Hastings "Jack" Skelly, Jr.
Born August 4, 1841
Gettysburg, Pennsylvania
Died July 12, 1863
Winchester, Virginia
Buried in the Lutheran Cemetery in Winchester, Virginia
Reinterred in the Evergreen Cemetery in Gettysburg, Pennsylvania in November 1864

Jack Skelly's grave

Jack Skelly marker

Charles Edwin Skelly
Born ??
Died 1913
Married – Susan E. Craver, August 27, 1863

Mary Virginia "Jennie" Wade
Born May 21, 1843
Gettysburg, Pennsylvania
Died July 3, 1863
Buried in the Evergreen Cemetery in Gettysburg,
Pennsylvania

Jennie Wade's grave

Esaias Jesse Culp
Born June 12, 1808
Married – Margaret Ann Sutherland October 16, 1828
Married – Martha G. Creager July 21, 1859
Died June 7, 1861
Buried in the Evergreen Cemetery in Gettysburg, Pennsylvania

Margaret Ann Sutherland Culp
Born October 5, 1807
Died November 7, 1856
Buried in the Evergreen Cemetery in Gettysburg, Pennsylvania

Henry Kyd Douglas
Born 1838 or 1840
Died December 18, 1903
Buried in the Elmwood Cemetery, Shepherdstown, West Virginia

Henry Kyd Douglas grave

Acknowledgements

Special thanks to Dr. James Price for his help in securing information about Wesley Culp's time in Shepherdstown. It was actually Dr. Price's talk about this very subject years ago that piqued my interest in this story. Thanks also to former Jefferson County Commissioner, Jim Surkamp, for his insight into the Wesley Culp story.

I am very grateful to Tim Smith of the Adams County Historical Society. Without Tim's expertise, this book would have been much less believable.

And kudos to Dennis Brant, author of the excellent book "From Home Guards to Heroes", who fielded questions regularly about the 87th Pennsylvania soldiers.

Much of the material on the Second Virginia Infantry came from Dennis Frye's excellent book, The Regimental History of the Second Virginia Infantry. Thank you Dennis for your excellent research on them.

Thanks also to Gary Gimbel, President of the Falling Waters Battlefield Association Inc., for providing expert information and an on-site explanation of that battle.

Thanks to my friends and supporters Doug Perks, Dr. James Price, and Ron Zeitz for reading my manuscript prior to publication and offering advice and constructive criticism.

Thanks to my steady and able supporters, who are always there for me, including my daughter Kelli, my son Craig and their families, my siblings and their families. Thanks to my late Mother for her love and support. And thanks to my extensive fan club.

I appreciate the use of the artwork on the cover of this book, provided by famed Civil War artist Mort Künstler.

A hardy thanks to all the staff of Infinity Publishing for backing up your promises with actions, every single day. Your support of authors like me is exceptional!

And a special thanks, again, to Rebecca Boreczky, who started me on the incredible journey into publishing.